Descent

THE IMMORTAL CHRONICLES

BY

SLOANE MURPHY

Sloane Murphy

Descent
The Immortal Chronicles #1
Copyright © 2017 by Sloane Murphy
www.authorsloanemurphy.com

Cover Design by Steam Power Studios | Edited by Katie John
| Formatted by Sloane Murphy

Descent/Sloane Murphy – 3rd ed
ISBN-13 - 9781723774614

DEDICATION

To my friends who believed in me. Thank you so much.
Without you, this book wouldn't exist.

Prologue

ADDIE

I walk along with everyone else, my hand holding Livvy's, my backpack on my shoulders. We have just got off of the shuttle to the Academy. It's so big, but I know I'm going to love it here. It's so green, not like the Nursery. All I've ever known is the Nursery, and I'm excited to finally leave – although, I hope I still get to share a room with Livvy; she's my best friend. I don't have many people in my life, but she's always been my best friend, and she always will be.

"Addie, isn't this place so pretty? It looks like a Princess's castle! We can have your eighth birthday party in the forest! It'll be like that book Mr Montgomery read us last year, *The Secret Garden*!" Livvy squeaks.

DESCENT

"It really is! I remember Miss Evie telling us about places like this from the Old World but I never thought we'd get to live in one!" I exclaim.

Miss Evie taught us all about the Old World, and how the humans used to be in charge before the Outbreak. After that, only the immunes were still alive, and the Old World was dying. That's when the Dark War happened.

After a bloody battle, the Fairies won and now they're in charge; the Demon King exiled to the ends of the earth, his army destroyed by the Fae and Vampyrs. Other History is one of my favourite subjects. I think I'll miss Miss Evie, she made it fun.

We're all taken into a hall and given a bag. Mine and Livvy's are black, but there's red, blue and white too. I see people from my Nursery, but we aren't the only ones who came here on the shuttle. I heard Mistress Ella talking before our shuttle left about how human children like me, from five different nurseries, were going to the Academy. Something about us, 'overtaking the species again'. I don't know what that means, but she didn't sound happy about it that's for sure!

The Head Keeper walks onto the stage at the front of the hall. She's one of the Fae; the Heads always are. Even if I hadn't learned that before, I'd know she was one of the Fae. Her long black hair sparkles in the light, and her purple eyes are so bright, it's as if they glow like fireflies. Definitely Fae.

2

Behind her, sat on a long table are the Heads of the eight Vampyr houses. They are known simply as 'The Eight' and they make up the security of our world. I'm unnerved to see them all here. Only two houses look after our part of the world so the others must have travelled a long way to be here for this. I didn't think today was that important. The Eight's main role is to look after the four royal Fae families. The Valoire Fae family rule us here, House Bane and House DeLauter are the two Vampyr houses here who protect them as well as looking after us. One of the Keepers steps up to the podium at the front of the room and clears her throat to quiet us.

"Welcome boys and girls to your new home. Welcome. This will not be like your last home. It will not be all fun and games. This is where you will learn, and where you will be evaluated for the next ten years. Here you will be prepared for the real world. You will learn about the history of our world, and of the Old World. You will learn the history, not only of your kind, but that of the history of the Fae and the Vampyrs, and yes, you will also learn about the Demons – and the terrible war that gave way to the new world. You will be taught everything you need to know, including how to defend yourselves and those around you. Slacking will not be tolerated; anyone who is not keeping up, will be punished. You will notice you're each in different colours – these are your house colours.

DESCENT

Do not fail your house; they are now your brothers and sisters.

Now follow your house leaders, who will take you to your new bunks. Take today to unpack and get acquainted. Your schedules will be on your pillows. Tomorrow, the rest of your life begins."

Excited chatter skitters through the hall and Livvy pulls my hand in excitement. People start to move. Then one of The Eight steps forward. I can't help but stare at him; he looks so different to the Vampyrs I'm used to seeing. He has kind of long, black hair that falls into his eyes, but not so long it touches his shoulders. They're the brightest blue eyes I've ever seen. His cold penetrating stare is fear inducing. I seriously hope I never have to speak to him.

The room suddenly fills with his voice, and it's just as cold as his eyes. "Children, my name is Xander Bane; I am Head of House Bane. These next ten years could be the most important ones of your lives, so do not waste them." His words sound different to the way everyone else says them, he sounds like one of the Keepers from my Nursery who said he was from England. "Take the time to better yourself; to learn about our histories, and how not to repeat the mistakes of those that came before us. The actions you take here will reflect on you for the rest of your life. Your evaluations will deem what you do for your time here on earth. As humans, that time is much shorter than most, which makes it that bit more special. Try as hard as you can to make a difference." His voice booms across the hall. Everyone else is so quiet that behind his voice, you could hear a pin drop. "Remember this day. It could be what makes the difference. You're excused."

He steps back and the hall erupts into movement as people head towards their houses. I'm in House Black with Livvy, thank goodness! I don't know what I'd do without Livvy. She's *my* Livvy!

Once we're in the common room, we're split into four groups and taken down different corridors by the head of House Black. Her name is Keeper Kaylee and she seems nice enough. Livvy clings to my arm. I think she's as scared as I am that they'll separate us. I don't even think I could sleep if she wasn't in the room. It would just be... weird.

"These will be your dorm rooms for your time here at the Academy," Keeper Kaylee says. "These rooms and the common room will be your home. Respect them. Other than that, decorate them how you like. You will be sharing rooms, two to a room. Your names are on the doors. I'll leave you all to unpack and get to know each other. You might not be paired up with someone you already know, so use this opportunity to get to know each other. Tomorrow, the hard work begins," Keeper Kaylee says before leaving us to find our rooms.

DESCENT

Livvy holds my hand tightly as we wander down the corridor, looking for our names. We come to the last three rooms, one is the communal bathroom, and two are dorm rooms. We squeal delightedly at the same time – we're together! Yes! Throwing open the door, we walk into the room. It's so big! The vast window looks out onto the forest behind the Academy and I know immediately that I will be spending many hours gazing at it from the cute window seat. The room is sparsely furnished, just a bed, which is thankfully bigger than the one at the Nursery, and a desk with a chair; although it does have a TV. *We have our own TV!* I love the Academy.

Livvy walks over to the cushion-full window seat, and sinks onto the nook calling, "Can I have the left bed, Addie? Just like before?" Her big green eyes look at me and I can deny her nothing. I have always felt like I have to look after Livvy; she's so small – even smaller than me.

"Of course you can, Livvy. You can have whatever you want."

She glances out of the window and I can feel her mood sink. "Not everything," she says. Her eyes water and I wrap her up in a hug. I know the day has surfaced thoughts about her parents. They died last year, leaving her on her own – except for me. I was sad when they died; they were like parents to me. They made me feel loved, and since my own parents had not loved me enough to keep me, it was nice. But I had learned early that people always leave. The day Livvy's parents died, I vowed I'd never let her down; I'd always protect her from the bad people in the world.

"At least we'll always have each other. You're my sister and my best friend."

"You promise, Addie?

"I swear it Livvy. I'll always look after you."

A knock at the door announces two gangly boys, who stand in the doorway awkwardly when I throw open the door. One is taller than the other. He is topped with dirty blonde hair and looks like he's up to no good. The shorter, has brown hair with dark green eyes, which twinkle in the low light.

"Hi," the taller one says, "I'm Tyler, and this is Logan. We're in the room across the hall from you, and we decided we should all be friends. After all, girls need looking after," he says, looking proud of himself. Logan looks like he wants to be anywhere but here.

"Oh really?" I chide. "Because I think girls can look after themselves just fine, thank you very much. Maybe we don't want to be your friends." I cross my arms and stick my tongue out.

"Addie! Don't be so rude! I'm sorry, Tyler, Logan." Livvy looks at me like I just stole the last cookie from her. Stupid boys.

"Ugh, fine. Come in. I guess we can be friends," I say sulkily. "I'm Adelaide, and this is Olivia, but you can call me Addie, and this is Livvy. If you hurt her though, I'll bite you." I stare at them so they know I'm serious. I'm not scared of them – or anybody.

Logan is suddenly blurting out a compliment, "You have really bright eyes! I've never seen anyone with eyes like yours!"

I don't know what his game is. "Aaand?" I ask.

"Nothing." He blushes so red that I can almost feel the heat off him. "Sorry I said that," he stammers.

Tyler laughs and throws himself down on the battered sofa, which I had almost overlooked, what with it being tucked in the gloom of the corner. Logan still stands in the doorway looking awkward until Livvy brings him in and sits him down on the sofa, too. Boy, these dudes are going to be a pain in the butt. Not wanting to get too cosy, I sit down on the floor and ask them about their Nursery. Tyler tells us all about how he wants to be part of the Red Guard when he grows up, just like his dad; and how he wants to protect us from the Demons and the Shades. I think I might like to be part of the Red Guard, too. That way, I could keep my promise to Livvy and always keep her safe. The idea of Demons and the bad Vampyrs scare me, but that's what the Academy is for; to teach us how to fight them.

"I want to be in the Red Guard when I grow up, too!" I announce. Livvy looks horrified, and so does Tyler.

"But you're a girl!" he says.

My declaration has made Livvy agitated. "Addie, that sounds really dangerous. Maybe you should be a teacher, that's what I want to be, like my mommy was."

"Nope, I've decided. I want to be in the Red Guard. Just you watch. I'll show you I can do it!" I'm almost shouting. I hate being told I can't do something; it just makes me want it more. I'll prove them wrong. Stupid Tyler. Just because I'm a girl, doesn't mean I can't be in the guard. I mean, yeah sure, there's no girls in the guard now, but that doesn't mean I can't change the rules!

DESCENT

Chapter One

ADDIE

Ten Years Later

I literally cannot wait for this year to be done. I have a month of my Evals coming up, and then, I hope to any sort of power that's listening, I make it into the Red Guard. I have worked my ass off for the past ten years to be the top of my Defence, Strategy and History classes. I'm fully aware this makes me an outcast – but screw everybody else. Just because they want to colour in the lines, why the hell should I? The only people who haven't abandoned me are my three closest friends; Livvy, Tyler and Logan, who have been there for longer than I can remember. They don't care if I want to break the rules, they love me anyway. Hell, Tyler has even trained with me pretty much every single day since we first met. I'm sure he regrets it

11

now that I'm top of the class, but a girl's got to do what a girl's got to do! However, just the thought of my Home Economic Eval gives me shivers. A cook, cleaner or seamstress I am not. I still have to pass it though. Holy cheesits, that's going to be a sucky day!

"Cheer up, buttercup, it can't be all bad." Livvy floats into the room and drops onto the bed beside me. She's always so happy and cheery, that it's normally infectious. But before six thirty in the morning, and with no coffee in sight, I'm about as cheery as I'm going to get. I groan as she opens the curtains, and drifts around, getting her things together. She has her standard black Defence uniform on, but somehow she makes it seem so girly. It's a black bodysuit with grey highlights for crying out loud. I'm just thankful we're the black house. Wearing red, blue or white every day for Defence would seriously get to me. I like black, it's stealthy. Plus, underneath it all, I'm a girl, and black hides stuff!

I get up, grab my shower stuff and head to the bathroom. The hot water is glorious and it is the only reason I get up at ass o'clock. Sometimes, the hot water runs out, and I do *not* do cold showers. I wash my long dark hair, and then condition it. Thank god some things are still available from the Old World! Once I'm done, I stand under the hot water letting my muscles relax for a while; I took a beating in Defence yesterday and I can feel it. Noah finally got the upper hand after five years, and pinned me. It'll never happen again. What he doesn't realise, because he's too busy gloating, is I let him do it so I could see his technique. He's narrow-minded. He does everything the same way every time. He doesn't alter his technique depending on his opponent. That's why he'll never be in the Red Guard. He's too predictable, too arrogant – and that's why I'm going to kick his tall ass today.

Begrudgingly, I leave the stream of hot water as I hear people begin to filter in. I dash to my room and close the door, moving over to the dresser, which used to be Livvy's desk – but she prioritised. She works at my desk if she has actual work to do, which doesn't seem very often. We've accumulated so much stuff over the years, that it's not perfect but it works for us. I sit down and begin to blow out my raven hair. It's naturally wavy, which annoys me, but I've come to appreciate that the Old World had some brilliant inventions. Thank God for the vanity of the Fae and Vampyrs, who have made sure hair dryers and straighteners are still a commonplace object. Once dry, I straighten it, before putting it up into a sleek ponytail. It's gotten so long now, that even when it is up, it hangs down to my waist. But even though it whips around in combat practice, I don't want to cut it off. I love my hair. It's the only girly thing about me. I look at my reflection in the mirror. My eyes are so big, they're my favourite thing about me. They're a bright grey, almost silver, which is

13

unheard of for a human – but they pop against my ivory skin. At five foot three, everyone thinks I should be a pushover, another reason I work as hard as I do. I get dressed in my jumpsuit, and am thankful for my petite but curvy frame. Thanks to all of my training, my legs are lean, like the rest of me.

I do my morning stretches and realise Livvy has disappeared. She'll be back before we have to head to class. We have Basics this morning, which is dull as dull can be, but she enjoys it, plus we have our Eval for it this morning. Then Defence class after lunch. Defence is the only class not taught by a human Keeper. Dimitri is a Vampyr, and one of the Elite Guard Enforcers from House Bane. He is by far, the coolest and most down to earth Vampyr I've ever met. I have no idea what he did to end up teaching here, but he's been here since the beginning, and he encourages me to try for the Red Guard; the official enforcers made up of everyone, including, Fae, Vampyrs, humans, and the wolves.

There aren't many wolves in the ranks as the packs tend to keep to themselves on the outskirts of the cities, or so I'm told. I've never actually met a wolf, but the Red Guard is the highest honour a human can be given. We're made equal to one of the higher races and Protectors of the Keep. I have no idea what I'll do if I don't get in. I mean, I know I'll just be given my career path and marched off, but I don't know if I have it in me to do anything else. I don't exactly like being told what to do.

"Addie, come on it's time to go. I got you coffee"

"I love you, Liv, don't you go anywhere. I don't know what I'd do without you." I joke, but it's true. She's been around forever, she's like the other half of me.

"I'm not going anywhere, silly. You're my soul sister. I couldn't function without you. A bit like you don't function without coffee!" She laughs at herself, and probably at me, too. "Now come on, we're going to be late if you don't shift!"

I grab my stuff and head towards the door with my bag and my coffee. Tyler and Logan are already waiting for us by their door. It's our routine; they'll wait for us every morning and walk us to our classes, even when they're not in them.

"Morning, Sunshine," Tyler laughs and pulls on my ponytail. I slap him upside the head but he runs ahead still laughing. Mornings aren't exactly my strong suit.

"If I'd had my coffee, I'd make you regret that; I'll just save it for later." I wink at him with a devious smile. His smile drops for a second then returns. He knows I'm not coming for him today. I have to deal with Noah.

"Morning, Logan. Sorry, that idiot makes me grumpier than normal. You okay?" I ask. He's been quiet the past few days. I think he's nervous about the Evals, but I'll be damned if he'll tell me a thing. Ever since Livvy started

15

dating Peter, Logan's' retreated. I knew he liked her, I guess I just didn't realise how much. And Livvy, well she's clueless, and head over heels for Peter. No idea why. I think he's a total douche-monkey, but if she's happy, then I can put up with his lame ass.

"Yeah, I'm fine. Just distracted ya know. These Evals are going to kick my ass." He shrugs it off, but I can see the worry in his eyes.

"Oh, come on, dimples." I bump into his arm and give him half a hug. "You've got this. You'll see." He smiles, and those infamous dimples come out. He's grown up a lot since that first day when he was an awkward little boy stood in my doorway. Now, he's a lean, muscled, tree of a man. His sandy brown hair is cut short on the sides and longer on top. I'm sure he only keeps it that way so he can run his hands through it when he's stressed. His dark green eyes are flecked with brown, and they look old. They make the girls fall all over him – all except the one he wants. He wraps an arm around my shoulders and pulls me close.

"Careful, Addie, someone might think you're actually being nice," Logan chuckles as he teases me. It's common knowledge I'm not the friendliest of people to those outside of my circle. I've learned the hard way that ninety percent of the population suck; humans, Vampyrs and Fae alike. It's easier just not to let people in. It helps me focus.

"Ha ha, you're funny. No-one would ever mistake me for nice, dimples, don't get carried away."

"Oh come on, Addie, you know you love us really," he whispers.

"Yeah, yeah but you three are different; you're my family. Anyway loser, this is our stop. You ready for the Basics Eval?" I ask

"Not a chance. If I walk out of here with a pass, it will literally be a miracle."

"Cheer up, Sunshine. What's the worst that could happen?"

Logan groans at my nonchalance. At this point, if we haven't got the skills we need, it's too late. We won't be leaving the Academy, and we'll be held back a year. The only person who wants to stay here is Livvy, and that's only because she's still determined to teach. I watch Logan wander over to his desk with his head down. I really hope he's okay.

I walk over to my table, which Tyler is currently sitting on with the biggest, goofiest grin on his face. Oh God, what's he up to?

"Tyler... what are you doing?" I ask cautiously. That smile makes me nervous!

"Oh nothing, just you know, getting ready for my Eval with my table buddy."

"Oh hell no, Tyler! Go back and work with Logan. I work best alone," I exclaim. He can't honestly think today

17

is the day to work with me? He jumps down from the table and takes a seat in the normally empty chair next to mine, just as Mr Fitz walks into the room.

"Take your seats ladies and gents. Today is Eval day, pair up if you're not already in a pair and prepare yourself for the next two hours of your life."

I groan as I take my seat. I don't know how he knew, but as soon as I see Livvy sat with Logan, I realise there might be more to Tyler's actions than I first thought.

"You're sneaky, you know that, right? You knew he was crapping it about today?" I ask him quietly.

"Of course I did; he's been a quiet mess ever since her and Peter hooked up. I figured he needed her today, plus this way, I get to work with the cheery delight that is you – meaning I might actually pass this Eval. We both know without you, I'm a total lost cause."

I hear the girls on the table behind us practically swoon at him. Just gag! I get that he's pretty to look at, but the way girls go stupid about him, drives me nuts. I forget how nice Tyler is underneath it all, mainly because he's normally just a pain in my ass. He hides this side of himself well, and now I feel bad for thinking the worst of him. Jeez.

"Fine, Tyler, you can work with me on the Eval, but if you screw this up, I'm totally going to beat you. You hear me?"

"Yes ma'am!" he replies smiling at me, like he knew I'd never make him go away anyway.

I settle in next to him while Mr Fitz writes on the blackboard at the front of the room, detailing the steps of our Eval. I get focused and start gathering the bits we need for our first step; sciences, oh the joys! And they picked Chemistry. I have no idea why. I'm *never* going to use this when I leave here. I head back to the table and start going through the steps with Tyler, who amazingly, actually seems to be taking on board what I'm saying. I guess he wants out of here as much as I do.

We work through the Eval faster than I thought we would, and Tyler is surprisingly helpful. Who would've thought? We're just about to finish when there's a loud bang and a flash of light, followed by a squeal. My head shoots up to Livvy and Logan, whose table is currently smoking. Logan's head is in his hands, and Livvy looks like she's going to cry. Oh man, I don't even know how they managed that. The entire class is laughing, and Mr Fitz looks like his face is going to explode, it's so red. I want to go to Livvy, but she looks over at me and shakes her head. She wants to fix it herself. It kills me not to help her; it's what I do. Tyler puts his hand on mine and I look down at our hands and then up at him with a frown. He shrugs. I guess this is his way of telling me to keep my ass in my seat.

DESCENT

"That's enough of a show for now, get back to your Eval, you have ten minutes to finish part one," Mr Fitz announces, his face slightly less red than it was.

I look at the clock and finish off what I was doing, as Tyler writes up the steps of what we've managed to do. Next is Mathematics, then Literature of the Old World. The bell rings to signal the end of the Eval, and I silently hope I don't have to redo Basics. I drop my head on to the desk. This next month couldn't go fast enough.

The bell rings to signal lunch and I don't think I've ever been as thankful for that sound as I am right now. All those all-nighter study sessions with Livvy had better pay off. I put all of my things back in my bag, and swing it over my shoulder. Ty waits for me, before we head over to Logan and Livvy. At least she has a smile on her face.

"Let's go and get some food," she says looping her arm through mine. "I'm starving!"

We all walk to the mess hall and queue to get our lunch. I love how cliquey the Academy is. This room literally looks like something out of a movie from the Old World. We might be split into colours, but the room is a sea of groups. You have the athletes; the ones who all want to be in the Red Guard. The book nerds; who mainly want to be teachers. Then there's the 'popular' group; a mix of girls and guys who, for whatever reason are at the top of our crazy hierarchy. I have no idea how they got there, but I'll put it down to them being the 'pretty people'. I grab my lunch and head over to our table, followed by the others.

"Well, well, well. I'm surprised to see you up and walking today, what with the beating you took in Defence yesterday. I didn't think I'd see you for a few days," Noah sniggers.

Man, I *hate* that guy. I don't know why, but he's had a problem with me since day one. So what if I can kick his ass. He needs to man up and learn to deal with it.

"Oh please, Noah, like you actually think I didn't let you win. Poor baby, it must really suck to get your ass handed to you, and by a girl no less, every single day. I figured your ego needed the boost," I throw back.

"If you say so, I guess we'll see later today won't we. You won't beat me again."

"Oh, Noah, you wound me!" I swear, sarcasm is an instant reaction to this guy. "Now go and stroke your ego some more with your little friends, before I destroy you. Bu-bye." I turn back to my food to see my entire table with their heads down, trying not to laugh out loud. My battle with Noah isn't exactly a secret. I hear Noah huff behind me before he stomps away.

DESCENT

"Seriously, Addie, he just wants to *do* you. I'm sure if you let him, he'd leave you alone. Or you know, become your undying love," Tyler jokes.

"That's just gross! Ugh. Not even if he was the last guy on earth. I'd rather kill off humanity than that!" I say with disgust.

"Oh come on, he's not that bad," Livvy pipes up in his defence. I can see it on her face that even she doesn't believe what she's saying. She's just too nice to say a bad word about anyone. It's just one of the reasons I love her. She's nice enough for us both. I make a noise and shoot her a look to tell her I know she's lying. She giggles and finishes her lunch.

"You could always put him off by dating me you know, Addie. You know you want me," Tyler says with a huge grin on his face.

"Keep dreaming, Ty, you couldn't handle me. I'm going to head to Defence early and practice with my *Sai*. Catch you guys later." I stand up from the table and dump the rest of my food in the trash, slam my tray on the side, and head to the Defence Gym.

There's no one else in here yet, so I head to the weapons cabinet and pull out the box with my name on; they're the only thing I was left with when I was abandoned. What sort of people leave a baby with a box of weapons on the steps of a Nursery? Damned if I know, but I was given them back when I left the Nursery, and I've worked with them since my first Defence lesson. I lay the box on the floor and kneel back in front of it, opening it carefully to look at them. I love working with my three pronged daggers. Using both hands simultaneously isn't easy, but it just feels natural to me. Most people choose to fight with a *Katana*. I get it, they're long swords, they give you distance, they're easier to learn, and they're good for offensive fighting, but these are special. I respect them, and they respect me back. Oh God, I sound insane, but I still stand by it. I get up and take them out of their velvet setting. They feel like extensions of my arms. I start to work through my basic stances and techniques, resting my forefinger along the blade. Not many people fight with *Sai* like this but they balance better for me this way. It's the perfect way for me to fight offensively and defensively, all at the same time. I totally zone out, so much so that I don't realise Dimitri is watching me from his office, until he clears his throat behind me.

"Getting in some extra training, Addie? I'm pretty sure you don't need it," he says.

Dimitri is my favourite teacher here, probably because he gets me, and encourages me. He gets my need to be part of the Red Guard.

"I always need the extra training, Dimitri. You know me, I won't be happy till I'm passed out into the guard. Until then, it's not good enough."

DESCENT

He laughs at me. "Addie, you've been top of your class pretty much since you started at the Academy. I have no doubts about you getting into The Guard. It'll be a historic moment, that much is for sure."

"That's what I'm worried about. What if The Eight don't let me in because I'm a girl? There's never been a girl in the Red Guard before. I don't understand why, especially since there are girls in the Elite Guard, and yes I know they're Vampyrs, but that's not the point. Or is it? Sorry, I'm rambling. Can you tell I'm nervous?"

"You've got nothing to worry about. Now put the *Sai* away. We're doing hand to hand again today, and I get the feeling you and Noah have a score to settle."

He smiles at me. He's all too aware of the competition between Noah and me, even if I don't understand it fully myself. Noah isn't even in the top five in our class but he's had it out for me from day one.

"That I do Dimitri, that I do! Maybe I'll just let Ty beat down on him like he offered," I laugh, shaking my head. We all know I'd never let Tyler fight my battles; it's not the way I'm programmed.

"Just don't hurt him too bad," he says with a laugh before going back into his office to prepare for class.

24

When I wake up, I can't deny the elation I feel that knowing Noah got put squarely back in his place yesterday. Today, we get the day off because it's D-day, or Donation Day as most people call it. Today's the day we all get to line up for an age in the medical wing, so we can donate a pint of our blood to the banks. Every single human has to do this once a month – it helps the Vampyrs stay alive, and stops rogues like they had in the old days just killing humans. So, despite hating needles, I'm all for it.

Unusually, I woke up before Livvy today. It's the time of year her parents died, and she always gets slightly sad around the anniversary. I've learned to give her her space, knowing that in a few weeks, she'll emerge back into the happy-go-lucky girl Livvy is most of the time.

I get up and dress for the day, pulling on my favourite skinny jeans and black t-shirt. I straighten my hair and put it up, before waking Liv. She'll hate it if we're late. I walk over to her and nudge her causing her to stir.

"Morning, sleepy head, time to get up, otherwise we'll be late for D-day," I tell her.

Her eyes pop open and she bolts up. "Shoot! I hate being late!" she screeches as she runs around the room getting herself dressed and ready.

How she achieves looking so good in such a short amount of time often amazes me; I'm exhausted just watching her. I pull on my black leather boots and leather jacket and join her as she walks out the door. She bangs on the boys' door to make sure they're up, too. She totally mothers us, but without her, we'd all be screwed.

Logan opens the door and mumbles some nonsense I can't quite make out, before they both shuffle out of the room.

"Late night boys?" I laugh. It's nice not to be the grouch for a change! They both just groan back at me, which makes Livvy giggle.

"Come on, you pair," she laughs. "Let's go and get you some food and caffeine before we head out."

They nod and follow behind us, as we head to the mess hall. I go straight for the coffee bar and get us all a round, knowing one of them will grab me some food, then work myself over to our table. I get there first and practically inhale my coffee. Strong and sweet, perfect! Ty drops down next to me with a tray holding two plates. Wrapping his arm around my shoulders, he leans his head on me.

"Aw thanks, Ty! You know just how to make a girl smile," I say to him, the sarcasm dripping. But really, I'm drooling over the plate; poached eggs, turkey rashers and a bagel. My favourite! He grumbles something at me about his coffee, so I pass it over to him as Logan and Livvy drop down across the table from us. I can't help but laugh at the sorry state that is half of our table.

"What did you guys even do last night? You look like death warmed up!" I ask

"Benny had the guys over and we played some stupid drinking game, Ring of Fire. I swear to God, never again! I feel like my brain fell out my nose, and my stomach out my ass," Ty replies, his head laying on his arms on the table, eyes closed. "Seriously, the light feels like needles in my eyes."

I can't help but laugh harder, which makes them both groan even louder. I see Benny and the guys come through the mess hall entrance, and Benny swaggers in our direction with a smile on his face, as the others head to get food.

"I'm going to guess Benny won?" I say, as he sits down on the other side of me.

"Damn straight, girlie. These boys should know better than to play with the master!"

I laugh at his cocky comment. He leans over and takes food from Ty's plate, and Ty pushes it over to him. I guess he really does feel like crap! The rest of the guys join us as we finish up, then head to the medical wing for Donation.

"Are you guys even going to be okay to donate?" Livvy asks. "I can't believe you'd be so irresponsible."

The disappointment in her voice is evident, and I'm really glad she's not talking to me. Disappointing Livvy is like denying a sad puppy. It makes you feel like shit.

27

DESCENT

"Oh come on, Livvy, we didn't mean for it to get so out of hand," Benny says as he squirms under her gaze. Underneath the swagger, he's a gentle giant really. The rest of them look just as shamed.

"Well, I guess there's nothing to be done about it now, is there? You boys just let yourselves down." She stares at them all and then starts walking again, dragging me with her as they follow behind, heads hanging. I can't help but giggle.

When we get to Medical, I'm glad of Liv's obsession with punctuality; there's hardly anyone queued up yet, meaning we should get most of the day to ourselves.

The doors open and we troop in each taking an empty bed. I lie back and close my eyes. I really freaking hate needles. I swear the nurses here are Demons, not Fae, it's like they get some sadistic pleasure out of it.

"Are you ready, dear? You're awfully pale, are you sure you're okay?" the Fae nurse asks. I roll my eyes behind my lids. I mean really? Do I look okay?

"Yes, I'm fine. Please, just let's get this over with," I grate out between clenched teeth. Did I mention I really hated this? I can feel her put the tourniquet around my arm, and I clench my fist. There's still something freaking strange about knowing my blood is going to be used as food.

"Just a small scratch, love," she says to me in that sickly, sweet voice.

She looks old for a Fae, like a sweet grandma should look, but I know really, she's evil. She confirms this when she jabs me and it takes everything in me not to punch her in the throat. Freaking Fae!

"There you go, just lie still for a few minutes and we'll be done," she says before wandering over to her next victim – sorry, *patient*.

As the blood leaves my vein, I can't help but watch the clear tube turn red, my blood flowing freely from my body and filling the bag. It's weirdly fascinating. When it is full, she comes back and unhooks me, eliciting a hiss from me as she pulls the needle from my skin. She ignores my discomfort and slaps a Band-Aid hiding the crater she just made in my arm.

"The cookies and orange juice are over there, dear; make sure you sit for ten minutes before you go anywhere, okay? See you next month!" she says cheerily before prepping the bed for her next victim.

I go and grab my cookies and juice feeling like I'm back in Nursery, and sit waiting for the others as they come over and join me one by one.

Benny is one of the first to gain his colour and his smile back. "I don't know about you guys, but I feel like making the most of this sun. Who's up for some football?"

I will never understand guys and football. How much fun can it really be, running a ball up and down a field? I roll my eyes, but I know Livvy will be happy to sit out on the grass and soak up the sun, plus, this way she'll be distracted. She's not said anything, but I can see the pain in her eyes. She beams a forced smile across the room as Peter walks over to us.

"Hey baby, you okay?" he asks her, wrapping his arms around her. I see her sink into him and nod against his chest. He leans down and whispers something in her ear, before tightening his grip on her. I swallow down the jealousy that rises inside of me. Their closeness and intimacy is something I never thought I'd want, but I can't help but think about it the older I get.

She looks up at him and asks, "The guys are going to play football; do you want to come?"

I flick my eyes over to Logan, knowing the last thing he wants to do is hang out with chunder-pirate Peter – but he'll never deny Livvy a thing. Peter agrees and everyone heads out to the field. Oh joys, this is going to be fun.

Chapter Two

ADDIE

"Hey, Addie!" I turn around to see Tyler running towards me, his backpack slung over his shoulder.

"Hey, Ty, what's up?" I ask. He rarely chases me through a corridor, so I figure it might be important.

"Well, Benny is throwing a party tonight and I wondered if you wanted to go?" He rubs the back of his neck as he asks me, looking sheepish.

"Erm, yeah, sure, I'm sure Livvy is about."

He blushes a little and coughs. Anyone would think he was asking me out. Ha! Yeah right, he's never thought about me in that way.

"Oh, yeah, erm yeah, the four of us can roll down there together. So we'll come get you at like nine? That cool?"

"Works for me. At least Livvy can't pretend she has homework this way. You know Peter will probably be there though, right? Is Logan going to be okay with that?" I still feel bad for him. Poor guy has had a crush on Livvy since we were like, ten.

"Yeah, he'll be fine. He'll have a few drinks and deal. Thank God it's Friday!" He woops, then nods at me as his boys walk by.

I wave to Logan, he's surrounded by Lukas, Nik and Marc. I swear, outside of our dorm, those lot are attached at the hip. Tyler hugs me and bounces over to his friends, leaving me to walk back to the dorm alone.

Livvy is already there, her headphones in, writing some essay; probably for our History of the Races Eval. I mean, how much do we need to know about how the world crashed and burned six hundred years ago? I get it, the humans messed up.

The Demon King wanted to take the world for himself and the demons, to rule the world and all its creatures how he saw fit, and the Fae didn't want him to destroy it. So they fought against him, and so goes the story of the Dark War. The Vampyrs divided between the houses. Those who joined the Fae, and those who joined the Demon King. The Fae followers now rule the world, and the Demon followers, well now they're soulless Shades; a disease, trying to destroy life as we know it.

No-one seems to know how the Vampyrs came to be, just that the Fae were here first. History used to be my favourite class, then I discovered my need to join The

Guard – to be part of something bigger, and Defence took over. I walk over to Livvy and tap her on the shoulder, resulting in an ear piercing scream.

"Jeez, Addie, you scared the pants off me! My poor heart!"

I fall onto my bed laughing at her, I can't help it!

"Stop it, Addie! You know I scare easily!"

She sighs and I sober, wrapping her in a hug. "Sorry, Livvy; I didn't mean to frighten you."

"It's okay, Addie. What's up anyway?"

"Oh, yeah, Ty invited us to Benny's party tonight, you want to go?"

She looks at me with her eyebrow raised.

"What?" I ask.

"He invited us both?" she asks.

"Yeah, of course, he said all four of us could go over together."

"So you've already said yes?" She laughs at me and I know she won't say no. "Of course you did. I don't know why I bothered asking, but I don't think he invited *us* for one second. I think he invited *you*."

"What? Why would he do that?"

She's losing her mind, I think.

She smiles. "Because he's been in love with you like, forever, you dummy! I don't know how you don't know this!" she squeals at me.

"Don't be stupid. He's Ty! He's not into me like that," I say, fobbing her off.

I might have liked him like that once upon a time, and Livvy knows that, but that's water under the bridge, isn't it? I'm so confused, but I'll be damned if I'm going to show it!

"Uh-huh, if you say so," she says, turning back to her work. "Anyway, I'm already going; Peter already asked me this morning. He can come down with us. I'll tell him to talk to Ty. What time are the guys meeting us?"

Great! I put a smile on and try not to show my feelings about Peter. "Ty said he'd be here with Logan for nine," I reply. "You know Logan's in love with you, right? I mean you say I can't see it with Ty, but that's just outrageous. With Logan, everyone but you can see it. He'd be so much better for you than Peter, Liv." Dammit. I know I should leave it alone, but I don't like Peter, he's an arrogant dick, and she deserves better. Her and Logan would be perfect together!

"Don't start on this again, Addie, we've been through this. Peter isn't a bad guy; he treats me right." She sighs.

Yeah right!

"I know what you think, Addie, but he's different when it's just us. You'll see it one day, and as for Logan, he's like my brother; I couldn't imagine him any other way. Same with Ty, it'd just be weird."

I shrug my shoulders. It's a losing battle, so I don't know why I bother. That's a lie – of course I do. Peter's a total player, and a total d-bag. I just don't want her getting hurt, but of course, she doesn't see it that way. I swear I'll tear him a new one if he hurts her.

"But you really should give Ty a chance, you know? He'd be good to you, and he's like your best friend, other than me. I mean, he already puts up with all your crazy." She laughs and flops down next to me. "He's not like Thomas."

I shudder at the thought. *Thomas.* Ugh, he is the worst kind of slime ball there is. We weren't together for long, but that sleaze deserved what he got.

"Come on, Liv, don't bring up Thomas, are you trying to ruin my night?" I laugh. He's such a prick. "Anyway, I know Ty isn't him, but I've just never thought of Ty like that. Well, I mean, not in a long time anyway. Even if I did, you're wrong," I shrug, and stand up, walking over to my wardrobe. "Anyway, what are we wearing to this thing?"

"I'm not sure who you're trying to convince, Addie, me or yourself. I'll let it go for now, but you'll see."

She bounds up next to me and delves into my closet. My Defence gear is moved over to one side, those black jumpsuits are practical, but that's about it. Luckily, over the years, we've accumulated a big selection of clothes. We get stalls here in the summer, when we have time off from classes and have credits to spend. Most people get theirs from their parents so they get more than we do. I just get a basic allowance from the Valoire fund, and Livvy gets hers

35

from the savings her parents had. We normally pool ours with the guys, who usually end up giving us more than they spend. Their parents are really generous, and I think they know the guys share with us. Our styles are totally different, but it works for us, and Livvy just has an eye for these things. She comes out of my closet with a pair of leather pants, and a red crop halter. I begin to shake my head until I realise it's pointless – this isn't a fight I'll win with her. I guess I'll be wearing my hair down tonight. I look at the clock and see that it's nearly six already.

"Liv, I'm going to grab us some food and bring it up here so we can get ready. What do you fancy?" I ask.

"Just grab me a sandwich, you know what I like."

I'm stopped by a knock on the door. I open it to find Logan on the other side with a bag of something that smells delicious, and two bottles of water. I smile at him.

"Logan, you're kind of my hero right now. Come in," I say grabbing the bag from him.

I pull out a chicken salad sandwich for Livvy, because we all know that's for her, and hand it and an orange over to her with a bottle of water. I see a cheeseburger in the bottom and worship it with my eyes. Yum. I look up and Logan's still stood in the doorway. I smile at him and he shrugs back at me.

"Don't mention it, bright eyes. I just figured you guys would want some food if we're going out, and I didn't see you down in the mess hall, so I decided I'd bring you something up. I'm going to go and meet up with Ty and the guys now. I think we're helping Benny set up."

"Logan, you're the best, and if you're already going to be over there, don't worry about coming back to get us, I'm sure we can manage the walk without getting lost." We both laugh knowing that out of the four of us, I'm normally the one who gets lost. I might be able to kick ass, but navigation is *not* my strong suit.

"Don't be silly, Ads, Ty would have my head if I agreed to that." Then he looks at me all wide eyed, like he probably shouldn't have said anything. He nervously tries to laugh it off.

"Yeah, yeah, him and his macho bull. Fine, we'll see you at nine, yeah?" I roll my eyes at him and his relief is evident.

"Yeah, see you later," he says leaving with a wave at Livvy, who just smiles back.

When I've shut the door behind him, I ask, "What was that about Liv? You're never that quiet."

"I don't know; I just didn't feel like I needed to say anything. I'm sure he's fine anyway. Now come on, eat your burger and get ready."

DESCENT

Livvy and I are finally ready, and with the music from our CD player up loud, I'm finally in the mood to head out. Music is one of the things from the Old World I'm most thankful for. The Fae and the Vampyrs really nailed it when they decided to remake the technology to play music from the Old World. The Old World may have been destructive, but they knew how to party. Music from now just isn't as good.

We're dancing around the room while we wait for Tyler and Logan to show their faces. I might not have been happy with Liv's choices for my wardrobe when she picked them, but I have to admit, I feel good. The leather pants are like a second skin, but they're worn, so they're easy enough to move about in, and the crop top shows off my flat stomach. I have a silver chain running around my neck that travels down my torso, attached to an identical chain wrapped around my hips. I have almost no makeup on, just some eyeliner and mascara to show off my long lashes. My long dark hair is down in giant curls, with some twisted gem pins run through it. She added a small braid with some purple ribbon, which goes all the way around my head, and over my forehead. Livvy really knows what she's doing with this stuff. I don't even feel like I look like me.

I'm spinning around to the music, my silver necklaces swinging wildly and the small braids Livvy has added to my hair, doing their own crazy dance, when I see Tyler and Logan just inside the door. I hadn't even heard them come in. I guess Livvy hadn't either because her eyes are still closed, as she's dancing to the music. The look on their faces is hilarious, and I burst out laughing. I walk over to the CD player and turn the music down. Livvy opens her eyes and starts laughing, too.

"Hey," I wave to the guys. "You enjoying the show?" They both blush, which makes me laugh a little harder.

"You two look amazing! Like, really amazing," Tyler says, his gaze roaming my body, then bouncing to Livvy, then back. "Like, maybe we shouldn't go out? We could just watch a movie or something?" He's rubbing the back of his neck and looking to Logan for some back up. Screw that. I want to party.

"Don't be an idiot, Tyler, it's just clothes. Anyway, I want to dance, so you guys can stay here if you want, but we're going. Right Liv?"

"Well, yeah! I didn't spend this long making us beautiful to stay in and sit on the sofa!"

She runs around, grabbing her stuff and putting the last touches on her face. I use the time to look Ty over. He looks good tonight. His jeans ride low on his hips, and I see that 'V' that makes smart girls stupid peeking out in-between them and his black t-shirt. He's wearing his beanie, pulled down over his dirty blonde hair. I've never noticed it before, but Tyler has grown up and become a man. He's always just been Ty to me. I wonder if what

Livvy says is true and standing here in this moment, I'm not sure how I feel about it.

"Okay, well let's head out then, Peter's going to meet us there," Logan says.

I hear the party before I see it. The loud, low beat of the bass from the music, the flashing lights. I have no idea how they've managed to pull this off, or how they managed to get alcohol in here. The fact that The Keepers haven't shut it down yet is amazing so I'm going to enjoy myself while I can.

Livvy branches off from us and heads for Peter as soon as she sees him. I kind of expected it but it still smarts to be abandoned so quickly. Screw it, I'm going to drink and have fun – even if I do it on my own.

The dance floor is tightly packed with writhing bodies. There's so many people in here, it's like the whole Academy came out to party. Tyler and Logan follow close behind as I push my way through to the kitchen, which has been converted into a makeshift bar. Benny is here and I smile as he struts over to me and envelopes me in a bear hug, lifting me off the floor and spinning me around.

"Hey, Short Stack, you look amazing! You're going to save a dance for Benny, right?" He winks and I laugh. He's such a clown.

"If you don't put me down, the only thing you'll get from me is a whooping." He knows I'm not serious but I hate being called Short Stack. He's done it for years. The fact that he's a seven-foot-tall beast is irrelevant. "You're giving me vertigo being up this high, Benny."

"Sorry." He puts me down and hands me a bottle of something; I've no idea what it is but I take a swig anyway.

I don't even realise Benny still has his hands on me until Tyler steps up to us and takes my hand, pulling me onto the dance floor. The song is hypnotising and I start moving to the beat, losing myself in it. Tyler moves behind me and wraps his arms around my waist. We meld together and I can't tell where he begins and I end.

His head drops to my shoulder and his breath is hot against my skin. I open my eyes and look at him. Our eyes lock, and it's then I know Livvy is right. Ty makes me feel safer than any other person I know. He's always there for me. Tilting my head to him, he leans down as if about to take me up on my invitation and kiss me – but I catch myself being an idiot and pull away from him just in time, smiling.

I don't want things to be weird with us, even though I can see from the confusion in his eyes that things have already gone there. Taking his hand, I lead him to the bar.

I need a drink! He follows behind and knowing me like he always does, he grabs me another bottle.

He sits down and pulls me onto his lap, cocooning me in his arms. I feel safe. He's so much bigger than me. Livvy is dancing with Peter but when she sees me and Ty, her squeal is almost visual. She's smiling like the damn cat who caught a canary. My smile matches hers as I lean back into Tyler, savouring the feel of his hot body under mine.

That's when I see Xander Bane.

He's standing across the room looking right at me with his piercing blue eyes, which hypnotise me for a moment. Everything stops. I don't see anything but him. He pulls his gaze from me, and man, does he look angry. I sober and sit up straight. The music cuts causing a ripple of groans around the room. Dimitri is facing off with Benny about the party. We knew it would happen – Benny's parties always get crashed but I sure as hell didn't expect it to be Dimitri and Xander who would come calling. Normally, a Keeper shuts us down and sends everyone home. Why would a member of the Eight and another Vampyr come here?

"Party's over, ladies and gents. I suggest you put your drinks down and head back to your dorms. Anyone who even thinks about protesting is going to seriously regret it." Xander's voice booms across the room.

Everyone's shocked. Why is he even here? He's meant to be at Valoire Palace. A few girls start whispering about how pretty he sounds, he's the only English guy they've ever met. Apparently he's *old* too, so everyone sees him as some strict English gentleman, with epic power making him the perfect guy. Personally I don't see it, but I've never been one to follow the hype.

"Now!" he shouts, and the room becomes a buzz of movement as people put their drinks down and start to head out. I stay where I am, knowing Livvy and Logan will come and find us so we can all head out together, but they're taking their time.

Tyler whispers in my ear. "Maybe we should head out, Ads?" It tickles, and I can't help but giggle.

"Miss Tate, Mr Knight. Move. Now!" Xander is looming over us, causing my stomach to roil slightly.

I stand up and Tyler follows, taking my hand. Out of the corner of my eye, I see them stare each other down, and I don't like it; it feels like I'm being claimed. Xander takes a step closer. He's so close to me right now, a slight lean and I'd be touching him. My skin tingles where I'm pressed between them, and I can't help the inexplicable sensations I feel. I clear my throat, trying to interrupt the weird display of testosterone.

When Livvy and Logan rock up next to us, Xander takes a step back although he refuses to break eye contact with Tyler. Whatever this is, it makes me feel agitated.

"Are you guys coming?" Livvy asks. Her question breaks the tension and Ty smiles at her.

"Yeah, sure thing, Liv. Come on, Addie, let's go." He tugs on my hand to pull me away.

I follow but look back over my shoulder at Xander who is watching me leave. Dimitri has joined him and is talking to him, but it doesn't look like he's listening. I shoot him a small smile, before tucking myself into Tyler's side and walking back to the dorm.

XANDER

She stood out amongst the crowd and I was drawn to her as soon as I walked in. When her big eyes zoned in on me, it was as if there was no-one else in the room – except for that pathetic boy, pawing all over her, making me see red.

She deserves so much better than some teenage boy. I hold myself back, knowing she doesn't know who I am. She doesn't know I've been watching over her for her entire life. Even if she doesn't know, I've been there in the shadows, making sure no real harm comes to her, stepping in where I can. That's the whole reason Dimitri is the Defence leader. I wanted her to train with the best, and other than me, he is the next best option.

I left Dimitri to shut the party down. My sole focus was on Addie – and that goofball who thought he could claim possession of her? He might as well have pissed on her – it was disgusting, treating her like something he could own. I don't trust him.

I try to calm the internal war going on. I'm torn between leaving her alone for her own good, and stealing her so I can hide her away. Neither sit well with me so I try and tame the beast within that tells me she's mine. At least I know she's safe here at The Academy. It's why I picked it for her. She doesn't know the input I've had on her life, right down to picking Livvy to be her roommate.

I watch her leave and it takes a minute before I realise Dimitri is talking to me.

"Man, you've got it bad," he laughs.

"I don't know what you're on about," I deny. "I just want what is best for her – and that snot bag isn't it," I growl.

He laughs again, slapping me on the shoulder. "Sure thing, man, you keep telling yourself that."

ADDIE

I hear Livvy squeal, and I groan into my pillow.

"Come on, Liv, it's a Saturday. Why are you awake already?" I moan. I miss sleeping in late, and last night wasn't exactly an early one.

DESCENT

After Dimitri and Xander broke up the party, all four of us came back and watched a movie, ate some popcorn, then ended up playing some stupid board game until about three in the morning. I glance at the clock and see it's only seven in the freaking morning.

"Really Liv, FOUR HOURS! We've had four hours of sleep. Ugh!"

"Don't be such a downer, Addie! Today is shopping day, and we can get our dresses for Prom!" she squeaks.

I moan again. God, I'd forgotten about prom. The idea of wearing a puffy dress and ridiculous heels whilst we all stand awkwardly in the main assembly hall, with cheesy Old World music on, fills me with as much dread as the boys who have to spend an evening stuffed into suits they'll never wear again. Prom is one Old World tradition I am not a fan of!

"Ughhh, fine! What time does the shuttle leave to go to the centre? God forbid they bring clothes here, like normal!"

"Addie! Stop it! It will be fun. You know they let us go and shop because it's a special occasion. Please don't ruin this for me. I'm so excited about finding the perfect dress, and about how amazing prom is going to be. I've been working so hard on the committee to make sure it'll be fabulous."

I roll my eyes. There's no denying the amount of work Livvy has put into making it all, 'just perfect'.

"Please just try, for me?" she pleads, and she's doing that look that she does – the one that I can't say no to. Stupid puppy eyes.

"Fine! But I'm getting something black, Livvy, I refuse, flat out, to wear colour! That's my limit."

"Yay!" she squeals, as she dives onto the bed and hugs me. I laugh at her enthusiasm, and if it wasn't so damn early, it might even be catching.

"Yeah, yeah, now let me up so I can go and shower. I do not want to go out there stinking the place up. Are the guys coming?" I ask.

"I haven't asked but I guess so. I'll go and check whilst you shower." She smiles and bounces around the room. I sink back into bed and psych myself up for doing the whole *awake* thing; all I want to do is sleep. I heave myself out of bed, grab my stuff and head to the shower room.

I can smell the coffee as soon as I get back to our room. Thank heavens for Liv! I sink it down in a matter of seconds.

"So...." she says to me, looking at me like she's going to burst.

"So, what?"

"Seriously? You and Tyler! Last night! Tell me EVERYTHING!" she squeals.

"There's not much to say. Well, maybe there is? I honestly don't know," I ramble. "He tried to kiss me but

47

that didn't happen because…. well, it felt a little weird. Maybe I just wasn't ready for it. But he made it very clear you were right – and no, I won't say that again, but yes, he is definitely interested in being more than just my friend."

"Yes! I knew it!" she squeaks, punching the air. "Well? Are you going to be more than friends?"

"Maybe. I'm just going to see how it goes. It all seems so fast."

Livvy smirks. "It's not *really* that fast, is it? I mean, you two, you've been friends forever – it seems perfectly natural to me, and everybody else."

I let what she says sink in as I dry my hair. Thankfully, she seems to get that I don't want to talk about it anymore. That's exactly why I love her. She gets me. I straighten my hair and put on my standard jeans and black t-shirt, then lace up my boots and grab my leather jacket. At least I can be comfortable while in my own personal hell.

"Are you ready?" Livvy asks from her bed.

"I am, are the guys coming shopping, too?"

She nods.

"Okay, well then, let's go," I say, grabbing my key and stashing it in my pocket along with our credits for today.

I open the door and knock on Ty's door. He opens it and I'm reminded of just how pretty he is to look at. I look up and see his smirk as he watches me checking him out. He lifts his arms to the top of the door frame, filling the space, giving me a better view of that hot body of his.

"Like what you see?" he asks, still smirking.

"You know I do. Now, get your ass ready for shopping because I am so not ready for today."

He laughs and shakes his head before pulling me in for a hug. *Sigh.* He really does smell so good. He kisses the top of my head before releasing me. I hear our door click behind me and Livvy joins us.

"Logan!" he hollers, which is pointless because he's only about eight feet away. "Let's go!" He grabs his wallet and keys and joins me and Livvy in the hallway.

Livvy links her arm through mine as she skips along the hall and down the stairs, dragging me behind. Outside, the sun is shining and it's a beautiful day. The shuttle is waiting at the edge of the courtyard, in the same spot we got dropped off on our first day here. Benny and the rest of the guys are already waiting at the door and they call out cheerfully when they see us. *Maybe it's just me who hates shopping!*

After being dragged through more stores than I can count and Livvy trying on more dresses than I thought existed, I still haven't picked a dress. Livvy has grown increasingly frustrated at me and our friendship is at the closest it ever comes to breaking point.

"Come on, Addie, we only have time for one more store, we NEED to get something in here!" she pleads as she pulls me into a little boutique, which is thankfully quiet. There have been so many people *everywhere* today and I'm not really a people person.

Livvy starts going through the racks and a sales girl walks over to her. They start animatedly discussing the upcoming prom and what the perfect dress looks like. I leave them to it; I would be absolutely no use to Livvy at this point.

I browse through a few dresses and come across a long black gown. It's absolutely beautiful, and I know immediately this is the one. I grab it and try it on whilst Livvy is distracted. The last thing I need is her over-reacting about the dress. It's different from my normal style but it's the only one I've seen all day that I actually like.

Once it's on I make up my mind instantly. When the sales girl rings it through, the price she asks for is only about a third of what the tag says, but I'm not about to complain. I hand over my credits; thankful I've got enough left to get the earrings in the glass counter, which will look perfect with my dress. Livvy is nowhere to be seen and I guess she's headed to the changing room, wanting to try another dress on before we head back to the store where she's put her choice on hold.

With all my stuff bagged up, I sit on the sofa and wait for Livvy to finish. She doesn't show me her dress either but I hear her squeal and know she's fallen in love with it. The sales girl rushes into the changing room and I hear them both gushing about how amazing it looks.

"Oh, Addie, it's perfect! I can't wait for Peter to see it! He's just going to die!" she squeals from inside the changing room. I don't respond because I don't need to. She changes and gets the sales girl to ring up her dress, shoes and jewellery. I stay where I am, and see her shoulders drop. She looks over to me and I can see the disappointment all over her face. I jump up and head over.

"What's wrong, Liv?" I ask. She looks like she's going to cry.

"I don't have enough, Ads. It's so pretty and I look just like Mom in it." I hand over what's left of my credits, and she hugs me in the tightest embrace she ever has.

"Thank you, Addie," she whispers.

I wonder about her dress. The only picture she has left of her parents is the one of them on their wedding day. It sits on the table next to her bed and she says goodnight to them every night.

"Anything for you, Livvy, you know that. You ready to head back to the shuttle?"

DESCENT

She nods, a smile back on her face as she picks up her bags and follows me out of the store. We're the last ones back to the shuttle, which is no surprise to anybody. We climb on board and take the seat, which the guys have saved for us.

"You have fun?" Logan asks. Tyler smirks as I flip him the bird.

"Oh, yeah, bundles," I say rolling my eyes. Livvy slaps my arm and laughs.

"She's exaggerating – as usual, it was awesome! I love shopping!" she says beaming, and we all laugh at her enthusiasm. As the shuttle starts back to the Academy, I throw my head back and close my eyes – I feel like I could sleep for a week!

Chapter Three

ADDIE

Prom night is finally here and I wish I could be as excited about it as everyone else is. God knows, this last week has been nothing but Prom talk, and Prom prep. There's a massive gazebo set up on the back field for tonight and the whole place has been strung with fairy lights. I don't get it, Evals aren't over, we've still got shit to do, and yet, even the Keepers are going crazy about Prom. The girls in the lower years who have been asked by graduating boys, are a nightmare – all swoony and big eyed with grins on their faces that would scare a kitten. They don't have a clue that there are more important things than going to the dance with an older boy.

I know I've always been different, I've never been one of *the* girls. I've always had a strong sense of duty. The feeling I need to prove myself. To be better. It's like a shadow that follows me, and so I push myself; the Red

DESCENT

Guard being my goal. So all of this prom stuff seems like a waste of time – but jeez, there is no way I would *ever* say that to Livvy, which is why I'm sat here looking at my reflection, not really recognising who I'm looking at, while Livvy is already down at the gazebo looking as beautiful as always, helping the committee with the set up.

I'm not entirely sure what it is Livvy has done to my face, but I'm glowing. The silver gem glued to the corner of each eye, twinkles in the low light of the room. My eyes look huge, and maybe a little lonely, the effect of the liner. I bring a finger to my plumped nude lips. *'Eyes or lips, Addie – never both!'* I smile at Livvy's wise words.

Tonight it's all about my eyes. The green gem hanging from the intricate, black lace hair piece, falls between them, and I'm almost dazzled by the sparkle. I don't think I have ever looked so beautiful.

I go to my closet and pull out my dress bag. I take a moment to fully appreciate the movement of the silk as I pull it out. Then I slip it on. It's the kind of dress that wears the owner rather than the other way around.

I smooth it down and walk back to the mirror, sighing deeply. It is perfect. The top lace panel comes up to my neck. With loops for straps, my back is completely bare. The skirt floats a few inches beneath my feet, so that when I lift on to the tips of my toes, it brushes the ground. I slip on the black heels Livvy left out for me, and run my hands down the dress, trying to calm myself. I can't remember a time in my life when I've wore anything like this, and if I manage to survive tonight without going ass over teacup, then the Red Guard will be a breeze. I laugh out loud to myself and my crazy thoughts. It's just a freaking dance! I take a deep breath and put on the long black cape, which came with the dress.

I'm just done fastening it, when there's a knock at the door and I smile. *Tyler.* I open the door and my jaw just about hits the floor, both Logan and Tyler stand before me looking more like men than I've ever seen them.

"Well damn, boys, you both look HOT!" I laugh. I can't help myself. Ty smirks at me while Logan runs his hands through his hair. Bless him, he embarrasses so easily!

"Not looking so bad there yourself, beautiful," Ty says walking towards me and wrapping his arms around me. "Just stunning, wild cat. I'm not sure I want to share you, looking like that."

I slap his arm and take a step back. Boys!

"Don't be stupid, Ty, and calm it with the stupid boy possessiveness, you don't own me, so therefore you can't share me. Anyway, can you imagine the fit Livvy would pitch if we ditched prom? Believe me, I've considered it. Let's get this show on the road," I say, grabbing my clutch bag and shooing them out of the room.

I link my arm with Logan and wink at him. Ty growls from behind and I look back at him innocently, smiling at the scowl on his face.

DESCENT

"Come on, you, too, hot stuff." I say, holding out my other arm for Ty. "I like the idea of being escorted to this thing, with the two hottest guys at The Academy on my arms."

They both laugh and we make our way out to the gazebo, which looks as tall as the dorm building we just left. There is a long walkway, lined with fairylight-lit trees running from the back courtyard to the gazebo. There's something about it that unearths a feeling of memory. I've seen this scene somewhere before but I can't focus on it – there's too much sensory stimulation.

We enter through a curtain into a reception area. It's almost as dark as outside, similarly lit by tiny, magical lights. Everything glitters. A Keeper, who is one of the teachers here at The Academy, is behind a desk, stamping each person's hand before they can enter. We get our stamps and move towards the red rope barrier which leads to stairs, covered in a rich, red carpet.

"This is amazing," I whisper excitedly. "Livvy and the committee must have worked so hard on this!" I climb the stairs, with Ty on my right, and Logan to my left. Neither has said much and I guess I'm not the only one who's apprehensive about tonight. The music sounds beautiful. We reach the top of the stairs and are met by Dimitri, who is guardian of a heavy, black velvet curtain.

"How does this…?" I've no idea how all of this fits inside of this gazebo.

"Fae magic," he answers, smiling at me. I'm mesmerised but not enough not to see the frown Dimitri casts at Tyler when he thinks I'm not looking.

Dimitri takes my cape from me before pulling the curtain back. The view before me is like something out of a dream world.

"Have fun," he whispers over my shoulder.

I'm stood here forever just taking it all in. It's a mini dark paradise. The ceiling is so high and clear, that it must be glass; the moon and stars magnified by it.

In the centre hangs a chandelier, which has the illusion of floating in thin air. Coming from it are eight massive streamers of material in black and white, circling the room as they come down and go over the banisters which make up the mezzanine floor we're currently on. In front of me there is a double stairway, one going left, the other right, down to the ballroom, because there is no other word for the round room in front of me. To the left are round tables with chairs, where people seem to be congregating with their friends. Dotted between them are more of the trees from the front, but they look like they're growing up through the wooden flooring. To the right, is a bar which is all lit up with the same little lights that seem to illuminate the whole place. To the back of the room is a massive stage with a full band set up on, which is where the beautiful music I heard is coming from, fronted by a woman, who I can only assume is a Vampyr. She is singing so soulfully it's heart breaking. I catch a glimpse of a shadow on the mezzanine level, and assume that is the Vampyr security here for the evening.

Ty puts his arm around my waist and leads me down left of the two staircases. Logan follows closely behind. We find our table where Benny and the guys with their dates are already seated. Livvy and Peter are so into one another that they haven't yet seen our arrival.

I concentrate hard on keeping my balance on the stairs, listening to the beautiful voice of a soprano who is singing something magical and otherworldly from one of the balconies.

Logan touches my arm and I stop to ask, "You okay, Dimples?" I can't imagine how he feels being here and seeing Livvy and Peter all over one another.

"Sure thing, Bright eyes. I just... I'm going to head over and grab a drink. Make sure you save me a dance tonight, yeah?" I can see the pain in his eyes at seeing Livvy, looking how she does with Peter draped over her.

"Anything for you, Dimples." I squeeze his arm before he heads off in the opposite direction.

Before I can get there, Livvy's in front of me. Just looking at her makes me want to cry. Now I totally understand why she needed that dress; it's white, with full lace sleeves. White satin falls in waves to her feet. She looks just like her mom did on her wedding day.

"Oh, Livvy, you look…" I say with a lump in my throat.

She hugs me fiercely.

"Don't you dare, Addie; you'll make me cry! Plus, you'll ruin the work of art that is your face right now. You look so beautiful. I hope Ty realises how lucky he is, because every single guy in here tonight is going to see just how beautiful you truly are."

"Don't be silly, Livvy – but you, you look just like her. They'd both be so proud of you."

She pulls me over to the table, where an old polaroid camera has been placed. She snaps a picture of us both, then begins the round of taking pictures of us all. Logan wanders back to our table, drink in hand.

I'm squirreling away a picture of me and Ty that I love into my purse, whilst she gets a Keeper to take a picture of the group. I don't know how she commands the willingness of so many people; she's just a force to be reckoned with. Before she hands the camera over, she gets a snap of just the four of us. I might have to find a frame for that one, we all look so happy.

The night is a whirlwind, and I'm having so much more fun than I thought. My dance with Tyler earlier was intense and I'm torn up about it, we seem to have gone from nought to sixty in less than a minute – and after... well, once upon a time I had thought about Ty being more than my friend, but he made it perfectly clear we'd never be more than that.

DESCENT

But then there was that moment at Benny's party – and his behaviour at my door tonight. My head is spinning. I don't think he knows what he wants. And neither do I.

"You ready for that dance you promised me, Bright Eyes?" Logan whispers from behind me. I nod and we walk over to the dance floor. The string quartet are playing alone and the song is haunting and slow. He takes my hand, and wraps his other arm around my waist.

"You know, Dimples, I never thought I'd see the day we would manage to dance like this without breaking bones."

He chuckles and his smile is wide. "I know what you mean; we never were the most co-ordinated of people – until Defence, then I think we've got that handled."

I smile at him as he leads me across the floor. "Thank you for always being my friend, Logan. I know I don't always make it easy, and I know it doesn't always seem like I appreciate everything you do for me, for all of us – but you're the glue. Without you, we'd all just be lost. You know that, right?" I look up at him. I want to make sure he gets it. I love him like a brother, and all I want is for him to be happy. I tell him as much.

"Thanks, Ads, but shut up before you make me blush."

I laugh so loudly that he tries to smother my mouth with his hand. I lick it and he pulls it away quickly.

"Gah, you're so gross! I wouldn't have you any other way!" he says lifting me up and spinning me around, making me squeal. "You know he really does like you? I mean, guys don't really talk about that stuff like you girls do, but I think he's been in love with you since the first day you told him to stop being a stupid boy. You should give him a chance."

I wrinkle my nose. Maybe he should have thought about that when he rejected me.

The song comes to a close and we're heading back to the table, when I see Livvy running towards the bathroom in tears. I leave Logan and chase after her. I burst through the bathroom door to find her in a crumpled mess on the floor, tears streaming down her face, sobs wracking her body. I sink down to her and wrap my arms around her tight.

"What's wrong, Livvy? What can I do?" I ask her.

"He... he cheated on me, Ads... I saw him with that whore! And then he tried to deny it and make me sound crazy, but I saw him! I just.... I can't believe... I thought he loved me," she gets out between sobs. I hug her harder, trying not to crush her under the rage building in me towards Peter.

"Oh, Livvy, he's an absolute asshole and he doesn't deserve you! I'm going to beat the living shit out of that cockwomble!" I say through gritted teeth. "Just wait here two minutes, okay?"

DESCENT

She nods and I help her up off of the floor, grabbing her some tissue to dry her face. I can't believe he's done this to her – especially not tonight, not when she's all dressed up like her mum and this means so much to her.

She pats her face dry and retouches her make-up.

"Don't let him see how much you're hurting. Believe me, that scrotum-sucking turbomong is going to regret ever making you cry."

"No, Addie, don't. I don't want you to get into trouble because of him. We're over, I just want it to stop hurting." She starts to cry again and I take her out to Logan, who is waiting with open arms to take her. I tell him what happened and his face clouds over with anger. I've never seen him look like it – he's absolutely livid.

I plan to get Ty, and leave whilst Logan sits Livvy down next to Benny. Just as I reach Tyler, I hear a scream from Livvy. Spinning around, I see Logan is on top of Peter, beating the living daylights out of him. After a shocked pause, Ty and Benny run over to pull him off of Peter before the Keepers get to him. Peter doesn't seem to be moving and for a minute I'm both freaked that Logan has killed him, and that it wasn't me who got do it.

I rush Livvy out of there, going back up the stairs to Dimitri, who is already waiting with my cape in his hands. He just nods at me as we leave.

We head down the stairs, where the boys are waiting for us. Livvy runs over to Logan and hugs him.

"Well, that was more entertainment than I was counting on!" Benny bellows, laughing out loud. "Peter's just lucky we didn't all find out at the same time or he wouldn't be walking now."

"I know, right! I can't believe he would do that to Livvy; she's one of the kindest souls alive! I want to beat the crap out of him myself," I spit out.

Ty squeezes me, kissing me on the top of my head. "Calm down, my little fire cracker. He got what he deserved, I don't think he'll be around for a while,"

"Let's get out of here," Ty whispers into my ear and I nod.

He fist bumps Benny and says, "Catch you tomorrow."

Then we leave.

Back at the dorm, we find Logan on our sofa, with Livvy curled up on top of him, asleep on his chest, she's all cried out.

"Hey, Dimples, how's she doing?"

"She'll be okay. She's just devastated at him betraying her like that. I can't think about it too much; it just makes me want to pound on his face again," he says getting up and lifting her in his arms. He walks over to her bed and tucks her in. She stirs a little but stays asleep. He brushes her hair off of her face.

"Thank you for being there for her tonight, Logan," I say, hugging him tight. "I know she appreciates it, too. More than you think."

He squeezes me back before letting me go. "We'll see you tomorrow, yeah?" he says heading to the door.

"Of course. Night, Dimples."

"Night, Bright Eyes."

He heads over to his own room leaving me alone with Ty.

"I suppose I should head out now, too. Did I mention how beautiful you look tonight, Addie?"

I smile at him and go up on my tip-toes to kiss him. He meets me halfway and sweeps me up, bringing me to his lips, he kisses me. I'm pushed against the wall, his body crushing me. I grab hold of his hair and kiss him back until I feel lost in him. He pulls away, knowing things are moving too quick.

"Night, wildcat," he says kissing me gently and putting me down. He leaves the room and I lean up against the door, touching my lips, wishing I was bold enough to call him back to me.

Just, wow.

That was incredible. But now? I'm here alone and I'm terrified. I don't want things to change but now they're undoubtedly going to. We've been friends for so long and I don't want this to ruin things, it's why I've been so hesitant up to this point.

I touch my lips again and sigh. Even though I'm afraid, I can't help but be excited. I've never felt like this before. Screw butterflies, it feels like I've got eagles fighting in my stomach! I think I could see us as more than friends: much more.

I've never thought about spending a lifetime with someone else before, but maybe with someone who knows me so well, it could be something I want.

DESCENT

Chapter Four

ADDIE

Five years ago

"Come on, Addie, it's your birthday. We should do something! At least let me make you a cake. You're turning thirteen! It's a big birthday, you can't just pretend it's not happening," Livvy pleads with me.

I hate birthdays. They don't mean anything to me. My day of birth was the day I was abandoned. Why would I want to celebrate that? It's not like I had a mum doting on me, teaching me about all sorts of things only a mum can, or a dad to protect me like a dad should. Livvy's lucky, she might have lost her parents, but at least she had them for a little while.

"I said no, Livvy. You know I don't believe in birthdays. There's no point to them. It's just going to be another day, and that's the end of it. Just leave it. Please," I sigh. I hate arguing with Livvy, she's my best friend, the person I'm closest to in the world, but I just don't see the world the same way she does. I wish I could, but there are too many bad things in the world to think it's all sunshine and rainbows all the time. That's why I want to be in the Red Guard, I want to keep people safe.

"Fine, Addie. But I think you're making a mistake," she says, storming off across the courtyard. I hate it when she's angry with me, but I'm not going to change my mind. I head back to our dorm and flop onto my bed face down. Birthdays suck.

"Addie? What are you doing?" I hear from behind me. I lift my head and see Tyler leaning against the doorframe. He's got his hands jammed into his jeans' pockets. I swear, all he ever wears are jeans, a t-shirt, and more recently, that stupid beanie hat.

"I'm lying face down, dreaming about a vat of ice-cream, what does it look like I'm doing?" I spit out. I really can't be dealing with people right now. I don't want to be mean to him, he doesn't deserve it, but I'd really rather be alone. "What do you want Tyler?" I regret it as soon as I ask. He looks hurt. I know he's just trying to be my friend; why does everything have to be so complicated?

"Don't worry about it, Addie. I'll leave you alone," he says, before turning around and closing the door behind him.

Now I'm alone and I don't feel any better than I did before. This sucks. Screw it – I'm going for another run. I get up and put on my Defence jumpsuit, my sneakers, and redo my ponytail before heading out.

I start round the back of the dorm building, and run the perimeter of the grounds. The rhythm of my feet pounding on the pavement with the constant sounds of my breathing, soothe me and I soon zone out. There is nothing more but the pavement in front of me, and the next step to take.

I round the corner and see the entrance gates. I keep my head up and focus on keeping going. As I get closer, I notice cars pulling up to the gates. Cars are so rare these days that it must be Head Vampyrs, or the Fae, although I can't imagine it would be the Fae; they never come to The Academy. I slow down and bend over, so I can watch from a distance. The gates open and the cars drive up to the main entrance. There are three of them. I watch as some of the Elite Guard climb out of the front car. I can tell they're Elite by the black and red of their uniforms. Then out of the back car climb two other Vampyrs, these aren't Elite, they're Heads. I recognise them from initiation, Marcus DeLauter and Xander Bane; the Heads of their respective houses. They all gather at the middle car, and out climbs a woman I've never seen. She's so beautiful. She has long dark black hair, just like mine, and her dress is bright red, but she looks so elegant,

69

like a dancer. She glances over in my direction, and I think she sees me watching her. No-one else has noticed me, but it feels like she can see right through me. Her eyes are purple; I can't look away. That's when I realise she is Queen Eolande Valoire. I look away quickly. Why is the Queen here? She's hardly been seen in the general world since her daughter died. I don't know much about it, it all happened before I was born – but I know she wouldn't be here if it wasn't important.

I put my head back down and continue on my run, not looking back. I probably wasn't meant to see any of that, and I'm not going to say anything to anyone. It's not like I know anything anyway.

I get back to the dorm and grab a shower before putting on my PJ's, and walking back to my room, where I find Tyler, Logan and Livvy all in their PJ's, too. They are sat around the T.V on the floor with cushions and popcorn.

"Hey guys, what's going on?" I ask. We didn't have anything planned.

"Well, since you didn't want to do anything for your birthday, and I refuse to let it pass without any acknowledgement, I figured we'd have movie night as an unofficial birthday party. Surprise!" Livvy says.

I should've known she'd do something like this. I roll my eyes at her and laugh.

"Fine, fine, but I get to pick the movie!"

Tyler and Logan groan. So shoot me. I have a soft spot for old word romance movies.

"I swear, Addie, if you pick *The Fault in our Stars* again…" Tyler moans

"You'll do what, Ty? You guys agreed to this, and since it's unofficially for my birthday, when I didn't want to do anything, you'll sit there and pretend you love it as much as I do. And just for me, you'll act like I'm not a total loser when I cry at the end." I stick my tongue out at him and he throws a cushion at me.

"That's it! You're so dead!" I say, as I catch the pillow and dive at him. We mess about for a while, while Livvy and Logan whisper to themselves. Then Livvy jumps up and leaves the room. I look over at Logan who looks as confused as I do. She bursts back through the door, cake in hand with a candle sticking out of the top.

"I couldn't light it, and I could only find one candle, but you needed an unofficial-not-your-birthday cake," she squeaks, with a giant smile on her face. I can't help but smile back at her.

"Thanks, Livvy, this is the best non-birthday birthday, a girl could ask for!" I get up and hug her, then pull her back to the floor where we all get comfortable and Ty puts the movie on.

DESCENT

The movie finishes, and like always, I'm tucked up against Ty, crying onto his shoulder. I don't care how girly it makes me, or if he thinks it's weak. Their love is just out of this world! I want a love like that one day. I don't know if I that will ever happen, especially if I make The Guard. I doubt I'll date someone I work with, it'd be too dangerous, and who else would put up with me? It occurs to me that might be the reason women don't join The Guard.

Ty unwinds himself from me and stands up, Logan quickly follows him and they say their goodbyes before going back to their room. Livvy is curled up on the sofa in a blanket.

"You okay, Livvy? I ask. She's been really quiet since the film started, and normally she jabbers through the whole thing.

"Do you think we'll ever fall in love like they did, Addie?"

"I don't know about me Livvy, but you? You'll definitely fall in love like that. Who wouldn't fall in love with you like that?"

"I want what they have. What they had in the Old World. I want a whole brood of children with a guy I'm crazy about, who loves me more than anything. I want to have them, and protect them, and love them because they're mine – because they came from true love."

"You'll have that, Livvy, just you wait and see. I can see you as a mum, with lots of little yous running around driving you nuts, and me, Auntie Addie, teaching them how to do it right," I chuckle.

"Never leave me, Addie. I don't know how I'd survive without you." She leans over to me, and I hug her.

"I'm not going anywhere, Livvy. Like I've always said, I will always protect you. Always." And I mean it – with every part of me. Livvy is so pure and so good, she deserves to live a long, happy life, full of everything she's ever dreamed of. God help anyone who stands in her way.

DESCENT

ADDIE

Present Day

"Livvy! Livvy, wake up!" I scream at her. The alarms are blaring, and I've never heard them go off before. This can only mean one thing; Shades are trying to breach the walls.

"For God's sake, Livvy, wake the hell up!" I slap her, I don't know what else to do. She shoots up, nearly head-butting me in the face. I jump back and rip off her cover.

"Addie? What's going on? What's that noise?" she asks, the panic all over her voice. Tyler and Logan burst through the door, making her scream.

"The alarm, Addie," Tyler says, panic evident in his eyes.

"I know, I know. Liv, get dressed. Jeans and tee, black. Now! Don't ask questions, we don't have time. I'll explain on the way," I order, trying to keep my voice calm. I have no experience in this, and everyone is looking at me like I have all the answers. Well, shit. I pull on my black jeans and vest, and throw my hair into a ponytail. No time for anything else. I grab my black hoodie, noticing the guys have already got theirs on.

"We need to head down to Defence. Dimitri will be there, unless he's already out with The Red Guard, and even if he's not, we need weapons." I look at them; Livvy is wrapped around Logan who is trying to stay strong, and Tyler has his game face on.

The alarm is still going off, and red lights flicker on and off in the hallways. I peer around the door frame, Livvy is behind me with Logan, then Tyler is bringing up the rear. People are running around screaming, like it's going to help them; others don't even seem to know what's going on. I step out into the hall, and start making my way slowly down the hall, keeping an eye on everyone else. I can see Tyler rounding people up as we go, so our foursome ends up turning into half of our floor. God knows where the rest of them are already. I try to think of a way to get to the Defence room without going through the courtyard, but I can't think of a way around it. I lock eyes with Tyler and know he's just realised the same thing. We're going to have to split up, the space is too open, and walking through it in such a big group would be like shooting fish in a barrel. We're just asking to be picked off.

Shit, shit, shit! I start down into the stairwell. We've got to get down four flights of stairs, before the alley to the court yard. Across that to the fountain, and then we should be good to the Defence room.

I open the door to the stairwell and signal to Livvy to wait a second, whilst I make sure the coast is clear. Why the hell are the Shades attacking? It makes no sense. The only place more guarded than The Academy, is the Fae palace. I creep out into the stairwell. I can hear my heartbeat in my ears. The alarm is screaming, making it hard to judge what's going on. I look down the middle of the stairwell, and the flashing red emergency lights make it hard to see anything. Screw it. We've got this. We've only got to make it a couple of hundred meters.

I walk back to the door and signal to Tyler that we're clear, then head back to the front. I wish I had my *Sai* already. I'd feel so much better about this if I did. I take a deep breath, and start down the stairs. I get to the bottom floor and release a breath to try and calm myself. I look behind me and see the group Tyler has managed to accumulate. He's added people from each floor as we've come down. Not one of these people are fighters. God dammit! I feel responsible for each and every single one of them. Tyler stands at the top of the flight of stairs. I can see the worry in his eyes reflecting my own, not that I'd expect anyone else to notice. He's like me – they'll only see what he wants them to see. I know he lets me in.

DESCENT

I take a deep breath and slowly open the entrance door. It's so dark outside, but I can hear screams, and I can see smoke and fire.

"Fuck!" I whisper. Tyler rushes down the stairs towards me. I guess I wasn't as quiet as I thought.

"The Tower's on fire. It looks like it's spreading into the main hall." I look up and meet his eyes. "Tyler, if it reaches there…"

"I know, Addie. One problem at a time. First the courtyard, then we'll worry about the fire. Okay?" He reaches up and cups my chin making me keep eye contact with him. His faith in me floors me, he really thinks we can do this. He thinks *I* can do this.

I steal some of his strength in that moment. *Come on, Addie. We've got this.* I square my shoulders and nod at him to let him know I'm good. I head out of the door as he directs people to be quiet, and to follow me. I hug the wall as I turn left out of the dorm, then run across the green. I look back to make sure Livvy is keeping up. Once I reach the alley that leads to the courtyard, I lean against the fence waiting for everyone to catch up.

In the time it takes Tyler to make sure everyone is with us, the screams have got louder and closer. I see someone running out of the White House dorm screaming, and I see a shadow chasing her.

Shades!

I look to Tyler and I know he's seen it, too. They're gaining on us. I grab Livvy's hand and turn, running down the alley as quickly and quietly as I can. She starts to cry. I want to comfort her but we don't have time; we need to get to safety. Once we're there, I can make sure she's okay. I can hear people running through the courtyard, and it makes me nervous about getting us all across to the Defence building. It's such an open space, and it wasn't designed with security in mind.

I signal back to Tyler that I'm going forward, and he nods to let me know he understands. He comes to the front of the line of people. He knows Livvy, Logan and himself are my first priority. I know it's the same for him, which makes me feel better.

I head to the opening of the alley and stop to take a look at the courtyard. There are bodies everywhere, students, Keepers, Shades and the Red Guard alike. It's like a scene from a massacre. I've never seen so much death. I feel tears in my eyes and quickly wipe them away. I don't see any live Shades around, so signal to Tyler to follow.

I can feel my hand start to tremble, so I mentally shake myself. I need to stay strong for Livvy. What sort of Red Guard would I be if I can't handle this? I take another deep breath and steel myself against what I know I'm about to see, then head out into the courtyard, stepping over and around the bodies of the fallen. I hear Livvy gasp and Tyler swear under his breath, but I try not to pay attention as I navigate across the open space.

I'm nearly half way when I see a group of Shades to the right. They're coming straight towards us, and we're just out in the open. I know the others have spotted them when I hear a girl scream from the back of the group. I grab Livvy's arm and start to run towards to the fountain. I can hear Tyler and Logan close behind us, their pace matching ours.

I get to the fountain and duck down behind it, dragging Livvy down with me. She's full on sobbing at this point; I know the fear is getting the better of her. Tyler and Logan crouch down behind us. I can see Tyler trying to work out if he can go back and save anyone, but more Shades have joined them and people are running in all directions to get away. I drop my head into my hands and feel a hand on my shoulder.

"Come on, Addie, we can't do anything here. We need to get to Defence," Tyler whispers. I know he's right, I just feel so frustrated and hopeless right now. I want to do more, but without a weapon, I'm as good as dead against the Shades. I meet his eyes and nod to let him know I've heard him. I get up slowly and all three mirror my actions.

"Come on, Livvy, not much further, I just really need you to keep quiet for a little longer okay?" I whisper. I don't want the Shades to spot us.

I turn and head to the building, I can't see anyone else around. I open the door, which squeaks and I freeze. It sounds so loud, and I'm on hyper alert. I don't think anyone noticed, so I head in and down the corridor towards the Defence room. It's so dark in here that I can barely see, but I know this place better than anywhere else on the campus. It's like my second home. I push the door open, there is no one in here and my shoulders drop. I had hoped Dimitri would still be here.

I go in and head straight to the weapons locker. It's already been raided, which isn't much of a surprise, but there's still some stuff in here. Tyler grabs a *Katana* from the wall and puts the sheath strap across his back, then unsheathes his sword. He takes a few practice swings to marry himself with the blade.

I turn back and kneel down to get the box that contains my *Sai*. I pull it out and lift the lid. They shine at me in the darkness. There are no emergency lights in here either. I guess someone cut the electricity to the building. I'm not sure how I feel about that, so I tuck it away to worry about later. I take a dagger in each hand and bow my head. I hope to God, or whoever is out there listening, that we all survive tonight. I stand and get a feel for my weapons, they feel like part of me, and I take slow, deep breaths preparing myself for what's to come.

"Addie, did you hear that?"

DESCENT

I spin to face Tyler who has taken position up by the door, Logan is with Livvy in the back corner of the room, trying to comfort her and keep her quiet. I head over to him and listen intently, holding my breath so I can hear any little noise. That's when I hear footsteps coming towards the room. Slowly but surely. I just can't tell how many pairs of footsteps there are. The pace starts to pick up, and we ready ourselves. It goes quiet and I tense. The door opens and I start to move before Tyler grabs me from behind to stop me.

"What the hell, Tyler!" I screech, then look and see Dimitri in the doorway.

"Good to see you too, Addie," he laughs, before his face turns sombre. "Seriously though, it's good to see you. I was worried when I didn't see you out there, and you weren't in your dorm. The Guard have the Black and Red houses locked up so they're the safe zone. You must've just passed them when you made your way here. I've just come back to grab some more weapons and take as many people back as I can."

I see the relief in his eyes at finding people alive.

"Sure, we'll head back with you. How did they get in? What do they want?" I ask him.

"They breached the walls, took out The Guard on the left side and scaled the wall. I have no idea what they want, but they came with a force big enough to wipe us out if they need to. I know we've dropped their numbers down some, but they just seem to keep coming."

I shudder. If Dimitri sounds worried, it must be bad. He's Elite.

"Have the Elite been called?" I ask. Surely someone got word out.

"They have, but they're not close. Who knows what they'll find when they get here."

"Okay," I nod. "Let's head out." I go back to the weapons locker, grab a belt for my daggers and tie it around my waist, then sheath my *Sai.* I grab two *Katanas* from the wall and walk over to Livvy and Logan.

"I know you both only have basic training with weapons, but you're going to need these. I hope you don't need to use them, but just in case, it's better to be prepared. Remember, stay close to us."

I head back to Tyler and Dimitri at the door, and prepare myself mentally for going back across that courtyard. It's going to be so much worse this time. Knowing the people fallen there. I feel Livvy grab my hand from behind and I squeeze it.

"We'll be okay, Livvy, you'll see. Just stay close." I force a smile. We both know I can't promise a thing but I'd die for her. I just hope I don't have to.

Dimitri clears his throat and signals to the door. He leads, then me, then Livvy and Logan with Tyler at the back, as we start back down the corridor. I could almost laugh at the irony of the fact we left the one place that's actually safe on the entire campus. The fire from the main building casts shadows in the dark hallways, a trick of light making everyone more on edge. We reach the main door and Dimitri goes through it first, with me following closely behind. The other three wait whilst we check to make sure it's safe. We separate and circle the courtyard, I don't want to get caught out again. I'm nearly at the other side with Dimitri, and I feel relief run through my body.

It's then I hear Livvy scream.

"Livvy!" I shout, turning to run back as fast as I can. We get to the corridor and I see Tyler on the floor, bleeding from a giant gash on his head. Logan lies not far from him, lifeless, his glassy eyes looking at me. I frantically search for Livvy, but she's not here.

"Addie!" I hear Livvy yell. It sounds so far away. I look to Dimitri and he knows I'm going after her. I see on his face that he's coming with me. I silently thank him and start down the hall with Dimitri on my heels.

That's when I see the blood smears on the floor. I swear to God I'm going to destroy those Shades. I push harder, following the trail. It leads to the Defence Room. Shit. All of the weapons are left in there; like we needed a bigger disadvantage. I steel myself as to what I might find on the other side of the door. I can't hear a thing. I push the door open and I can't see anything. Dimitri follows me closely. I should probably let the immortal Vampyr lead, but this is Livvy. This is on me – I should've stayed with her. Dammit!

"Hello, Adelaide Tate. I assume you've come to save this pathetic little human. You might not be in time, she's losing blood quite quickly, I needed to make sure she bled enough to get you here," the beast across the room from me says. He's obviously the leader of the group, but he doesn't look like a Shade. I can feel the evil soullessness coming from him. Dimitri steps in front of me to face him. Thank God for him right now.

"Kaden, fancy seeing you here. Picking on humans. This is a new low even for you. Now let her go before I make you."

"Oh, Dimitri, how I missed this. You really think you can win? You're precious Xander isn't here this time. You don't stand a chance," he taunts. I can see his minions coming out of the shadows surrounding us. Shit, shit, shit!

I look at Livvy, hanging there, his dirty hand around her neck. She looks so pale; I can see the blood dripping from her hand. *Hang in there, Livvy.* I need to get to her. I stand with my back to Dimitri, preparing to fight our way out of this, and unsheathe my *Sai*.

I face him down. "Oh stop stroking your fragile ego. You wanted us to come get her. Let's go bitches. Unless you're too afraid?" I say with more bravado than I feel. The Shade in front of me snarls and pounces. Shit, he's so quick! I barely miss him, and I just get the chance to see

Dimitri lunging for Kaden. Livvy is on the floor motionless, but I can't get to her. There are three Shades between her and me. I charge the first one, matching him blow for blow with my daggers. I shut down and become the warrior I've trained to be – step and slash, dodge and attack. I stab the first Shade in the chest, the silver destroying his heart, and he goes down.

I can still hear Dimitri and Kaden facing off, but I don't have time to think about it as the remaining two Shades attack simultaneously. Step and slash, dodge and attack, but this time I'm not fast enough. I take a hit to my stomach, which makes my breath leave. I don't have time to recover before they're on me. I take a blow to the back of the head, which sends me to my knees. Their strength is out of this world. I try to fight back, but I can feel how useless it is. I take a punch to the face and I hit the floor face down, before they kick me in my ribs. I can't move, and darkness descends, blurring the edges of my vision.

I can see Livvy right in front of me. She's still here, her hand reaches out to me and I try to do the same. I look her in the eyes, and a tear runs down my cheek. The Shades return to her, and I try to move.

Silently, she mouths, "*I love you. It's going to be okay. I love you,*"

I break. They took my *Sai,* and even if I had them, I can barely move. I try to push myself up to get to her. I know what's coming before I see it, but I refuse to accept it. I watch the calm wash over her, as they place my blade against her neck. "*It' not your fault, Addie,*" she says. I can't get past the lump in my throat, which has stolen my voice. I watch the life fade from her eyes.

I hear a scream; I think that's me.

She's gone.

I failed.

It's all my fault. That's the last thought I have before the world turns black.

My eyes flutter open. It's so bright, I have to squint whilst my eyes adjust. My entire body hurts. I try to sit up, but pain rips through my chest and I let out a small cry, as I close my eyes and lay back. The med ward is so clinical; so white. I take appraisal of my injuries. My wrist is broken, at least the cast on it makes me assume so. I can feel the wrap around my chest now too, either broken or fractured ribs. Other than that, I think it's just cuts and bruises. That's when it hits me.

She's gone.

She's gone and I didn't stop it. It's all my fault. I can't stop the tears. The pain hits me wave after wave. I was meant to protect her. My cries turn into sobs, and that's when I feel someone take my hand. I rip my hand away. I don't deserve any sort of comfort. I bring my hands up to cover my face as I try to stop the tears streaming down my cheeks.

"Addie," Tyler whispers. I look at him and see the pain in him, too. I can't handle this right now. I can't take on his pain as well as mine, but I can see how badly he needs me.

Logan's gone, too. He lost his best friend, too. I shove my pain down and lock it in a mental box, I can deal with it later. I take his hand and pull him on to the bed with me. He lies beside me. There's no more crying. Just silent mourning, as we both think about the people we lost.

I hear the footsteps approaching the bed and tense. I don't want to see anyone else yet. I look over Tyler's head; I think he's fallen asleep. The curtain at the side of my bed is opened, and I see a sorry looking Dimitri standing there with Xander Bane.

"It's good to see you awake, Addie. I wasn't sure when you'd come back to us," Dimitri says with a small smile.

"How long?" I ask.

"You've been out for about a week. You took some serious damage. You're lucky to be alive."

"Am I?"

"I'm sorry, Addie, I really am," he replies and looks to the floor.

"It's not your fault, Dimitri. It's mine. I should've never left her."

"Addie..."

"No Dimitri, it's my fault. Just, just leave it – please?" I ask him, silently hoping he'll stop talking about her. I can't take it.

"As nice as this all is, Miss Tate; we didn't come here to commiserate," Xander barks. His eyes are as cold as his voice. I hate him already, where the hell was he when we needed him?

"I can see that. What exactly is it you want, Mr Bane?" I ask. The bite in my words isn't lost on him, or Dimitri. I see him raise his eyebrow. I guess Dimitri didn't fill him in on my awesome people skills.

"You're wanted for questioning in front of The Eight, and the security council. We lost a lot of lives last week. Human and Vampyr, and from what we can tell, their focus was you. Dimitri mentioned that Kaden knew you by name. Have you met him before?"

"No, of course not," I spit out. "But I'd like to see him again, and make him regret meeting me." I am fuming. What the hell is he insinuating? That I had knowledge of what happened? He's lost his damned mind. Tyler stirs and Xander shoots him a look, and if they could kill, Tyler would be in a lot of trouble right about now. I'd love to work out what that's about, but I don't have time now.

DESCENT

"Well, Miss Tate, you might just have your chance. You're expected before the Council at eight tomorrow morning," he orders, then turns around and walks away from me. What a douchebag!

"Well, that went better than I expected," Dimitri chuckles, "Addie, you went easy on him, I'm shocked."

"Yeah, well sorry if my comedic repertoire isn't up to scratch today. I'm kind of broken right now." I don't mean to snap at him, but hell, I've been awake about twenty minutes, and life has got exponentially crappier since I did.

"How was it?"

I walk out of my interrogation from the council to see Tyler leaning against the wall, backpack slung over his shoulder. The way his jeans hug his hips and his beanie, just... damn! I take a second to really appreciate the sight, before I answer him.

"It was as spectacular as anticipated. I was asked the same question in a dozen different ways just to see if my answer changed. Like I say, freaking spectacular," I retort.

They really wound me up in there, it was like I'd done something wrong. As if I'm not already beating myself up about everything that went down. I know they could see it on my face, and even if they couldn't, well, they should have known better.

"Ugh, stupid Council. Stupid Eight. What do they know, anyway? It's not like they were here!" It frustrates me so much that they got here too late. "And why did they have to call on me so early, like we don't have class to get to. I need coffee, please tell me you have coffee?"

"Of course I do." He reaches behind me and passes me a paper cup, filled with the good stuff. Thank you to whoever created this in the Old World!

He wraps his arm around my shoulder, and pulls me close. He smells good today, too. Yummy. "How are you feeling anyway? Are you ready for the memorial?"

"No," I sigh. Some genius decided we needed a full school memorial to say goodbye to those we lost.

While in general I understand why they're doing it, I'd rather just deal with my pain on my own. Ty's not left my side since I left the med ward, he's crashed on the sofa. I can't bear to touch any of Livvy's stuff. It still feels like she's here – like she's just late out of class, or out somewhere with Peter. A tear runs down my cheek and I catch it before he has chance to notice.

"I don't think I'm going to go, ya know? I just... I'd rather remember them, just the two of us; away from the showboating of the Keepers and The Eight. They didn't know them like we did. I don't want them to be just another number, two of many who died. They were special, and they deserve to be remembered properly. Plus, the fact the Shades took so many bodies, and no one seems to know why. It just doesn't seem right memorialising them without a proper burial." I look at Tyler, and I see his eyes are glassy, too. He kisses the side of my head, then rests his forehead there.

"Yeah, okay, Addie. I think they'd have liked that," he sighs.

I turn to him and hug him, resting my face in the crook of his neck. He makes me feel so safe. I don't trust myself to keep anyone safe anymore. I already failed once. I don't want to fail again.

"Come on, let's go get changed and head to class," he whispers. I nod and we start the walk back.

Defence Class is our only class today, a full day of training. The Keepers and the Eight made the great decision after the attack that everyone needs to be fully trained in Defence, but still pass all of their Evals, just freaking great!

We get ready and head down to Defence class. There are more of the Red Guard stationed here now, and I heard they're having some of the Elite stationed here, too. I guess they really are worried about another attack.

I stop in my tracks. I don't know if I can go in there. I close my eyes and I can still see the blood trail on the floor. I can see her face as they killed her: The way she knew I couldn't save her. The sadness in her eyes that I'd failed her.

"Tyler... I don't think I can go in there."

He stands behind me, his head on my shoulder and wraps his arms around my waist. "I've got you, Addie, just remember, I'm right here and I'm not going anywhere. Just take a deep breath. We've got this." His voice is so soothing, and cocooned in his arms, I feel like the world can't get me.

"Okay, come on. Just, don't let go, okay?" I say.

"Addie, I'm never going to let go. You're all I've got." He untangles himself from behind me, takes my hand and squeezes it. "I'm not letting go. We can face this together."

I let him pull me in. As we enter the room, it goes silent. Everybody knows what happened in here, and that I was here when it did. I wasn't tucked away safe in a dorm house, or hiding in the mess hall. I was here, facing the Shades – and I lost. I steel myself to the looks and the whispers, and head over to the weapons locker, my hand still intertwined with Tyler's. It's then I realise I can't use my *Sai.* They used them to kill her. I can't. I start to panic, spinning to Tyler with wild eyes. He sees my thoughts and pulls me in close, stroking my hair.

"I can't do this, Ty," I cry into his chest.

"Shh, come on, Addie, don't let them break you. Don't let them win."

DESCENT

I know everyone's still watching me, but right now I don't care. I feel bad, because I know Tyler's hurting just as much over Logan, but I can't seem to get my crap together and deal.

"Addie."

I lift my head up and see Dimitri. He's opened the door of his office, and jerks his head to signal me to go in. I nod and unravel myself from Tyler. He shuts the door behind me.

"Take a seat, Addie. I know this has to be hard for you, but I need you to pick yourself up and brush yourself off. It sucks, and it hurts, I know it does. But we need to fight, and we need to win. Otherwise it was all in vain, you hear?" He looks me in the eyes. I know he can see how hard it is for me being back in here. I also know what he said is right. I need to deal, or at least pretend like I'm dealing.

"You're right, I'm sorry. I'll do better," I say. He stands and goes over to a cabinet at the back of the room, pulling out a shiny black box, then places it on his desk in front of me.

"For you," he says. "Go on, open it."

I open it to find, nestled in deep plum velvet, the most beautiful pair of *Sai* I have ever seen. They're black hilted with a silver dagger, and a purple stone laid in the top of the handle.

"Dimitri, they're beautiful, but you didn't have to do this," I sigh. I almost don't want to disturb them. I'm so glad my cast is off. If I'd have been given them and been unable to train with them, I probably would have cried. I've missed training with a weapon, and since my last ones were tainted and taken, I've not held *Sai* for what feels like forever.

"I didn't," he responds. "But they're yours anyway. Use them well." He goes back to his door and opens it, ushering me out. I grab the box and leave the room, heading straight back for Tyler.

"Oh look who it is, little princess warrior. Guess you weren't as good as you thought you were, huh Tate!"

"Shut your mouth, Noah," Tyler roars from across the room. "You weren't here; you were hiding in your room like a little bitch!"

"Tyler," I place my hand on his chest to stop him attacking Noah. "I've got this okay?" he looks down at me, and I know he can see the fight in my eyes when he smirks. He knows as well as I do, Noah is about to get his shit handed to him. I take my *Sai* out of their box.

"I can still kick your ass, Noah, now bring your little bitch ass here and let me hand it to you," I shout and fly at him.

I attack him before he has chance to work out what's happening. I'm on him. I don't hold back, and I take the full strength of my frustration and anger out on him. He fights back well at first, but once I slice the back of his knee with my *Sai,* he's down and we both know it. All I see is red, and it's not until Dimitri is hauling me off of him, I realise he stopped fighting back.

ADDIE

"Addie, Tyler. Wait up!" We stop and I look behind us to see Benny running towards us in a black shirt and trousers, his red tie shows his respect for of those who were lost from his dorm.

"Where are you guys going?" he asks once he's caught up with us.

"We decided to have our own memorial for Livvy and Logan, Benny. We didn't want to be around people who didn't really know them, you know?" Tyler says.

I'm glad he answered, because I'm not sure I'd have managed to get it out right now.

Benny's look is earnest, "Come on guys, you have to come. Plus, me and the boys want to say goodbye to them properly, too. And I know Peter wants to make things right over the situation with Livvy."

I can see my pain reflected in his eyes.

His voice breaks. "We all lost people, some more than others, but we're all doing this to be there for each other."

I can't stop the tear running down my face. I swipe it away. I've already cried so much; I don't want to keep crying. Livvy and Logan wouldn't want me to cry.

Ty looks at me. I know he wants us to go with Benny and stand with his friends at the memorial. Reluctantly, I nod. I don't want to be around everyone else, but right now, I don't want to be without him either and I know he really needs this.

"Yeah, okay man, we'll come back with you," Ty says. I can see Benny's gratitude in every aspect of his body.

Ty leads me in the direction of the main hall. I curl into his side as we walk and try to borrow some of his strength. When we get there, everyone is in their own groups, crying and hugging; I feel so distant from them all.

"Thank you, Ty," I whisper. "Thank you for being so strong for me. I don't know how I would've got through any of this without you. I feel so lost without her, Ty. It's like my soul was ripped in half, and I don't know how to get through the days. But you? You're my anchor."

He tightens his grip on me, offering me comfort, but he can't speak – he's too choked up and I can see he's embarrassed by the emotion threatening to spill.

"I know you're going through it all, too. I know you feel the same about Logan," I say through my tears. I can't stop them now they've started flowing.

Every morning since Livvy's death, I wake up and look over to her bed – and just for a minute, I forget that she's gone. Then it hits me and I'm paralysed. I can't move, I can't breathe while it hits me all over again, that she's never coming back. That's when I panic, but Ty is there every single time. He makes me feel something. He keeps the hurt away just enough so it's bearable.

"I'm here for you, Addie - I'll always be here for you. I promise," he says, pulling me into him and kissing the top of my head. And just like that, I can breathe again.

I stay there until the Head of the Academy announces the memorial is about to begin, and people start filing in the doors. Everyone who survived the attack is here, and while there are a lot of us, there's nowhere near as many as there was last week. I hadn't thought about the sheer number of people we had lost; I couldn't fathom it. But now, seeing everyone here together, the difference is overwhelming. Tyler takes my hand and pulls me forward with the crowd, and soon I'm surrounded by his friends as we filter into the hall.

We take our seats and I see Xander sat up on the stage. He's looking straight at me. I look around but no one else seems to notice. I look back at him and he's still looking at me, but there's no expression on his face and

DESCENT

I'm not even sure he sees me. He lost a lot of friends, brothers, too. Some of his house would have been in the Red Guard who were protecting the Academy. I turn away, the sight of him makes me inexplicably uncomfortable, and move into Tyler's side.

Different people take turns talking about those whom they lost. First, the Head of the Academy, then, the Keepers. Some students also speak about those they lost during the attack, but I'm numb through it all. I know these people are sad, too, but I can't be sad for them; I have enough of my own pain to deal with. I don't know how Tyler does it.

Xander stands up to speak and Dimitri stands with him, clasping his shoulder in solidarity before taking his seat again. I'm surprised by the depth of their friendship – Xander Bane doesn't give off the impression he *does* friendship. He walks over to the podium and grips it with both hands.

"We stand here today, to remember those who have fallen. Those who stood to protect the lives we cherish so deeply, and those whose lives were cut too short. But we also stand here, strong – in the knowledge they did not die in vain. They died so we might continue to live, and while we may be a little broken, we will rebuild, and become stronger than ever."

I'm hooked on each word. He looks straight at me.

"I know right now, you are in pain. It feels like you're lost – but there will be a tomorrow, and you will find yourself again. Lean on each other, lean on us, lean on me. I am here to protect you. Know that from this great tragedy, greatness rises."

I'm breathless. He is speaking to me, and me alone – even though the rest of the assembly can hear him, his words are not meant for them. Those words run around in my head. He's right. Her death cannot be in vain. I failed to protect her, but she would want me to keep going – to protect others.

After he finishes, he dismisses us and tells us we'll have no classes for three days, to allow us to mourn. But after that, in light of everything, every day we will now do half a day of Defence, regardless of whether were taking it or not. I smile internally at this. I'm going to need Defence to keep me strong.

Afterwards, our small band of friend's head to the forest for the mini memorial Tyler and I planned for Livvy and Logan. I have chosen the spot where Livvy and I would come to get away from things when they got too much. We would come down here and it felt like the rest of the world didn't exist.

Earlier, I came down on my own and placed a framed picture of the four of us and surrounded it with candles and wildflowers, which I picked in the forest. When I see it again, every bit of strength I just gained from Xander's speech leaves me. The grief washes over me in waves and it feels like I'm drowning. I can't believe they're gone. Losing Livvy is like losing my soul, but losing Logan, too? It's like losing my heart.

People didn't always get to see the real him, but he let me in. He opened up to me, and he made me feel special. He had the ability to make a person feel like they were the most important person in the room. I feel so lost without them – like without them, I'm not even me anymore. It's not just that they're gone, it's all the things we'll never get to do. We'll never be able to take pictures like that again. What if, over time, I forget what they look like? I fall to the floor in front of the memorial, and the guys sit down around me. I know they do that for me, I must look like a complete mess.

They start talking memories of Logan and Livvy; recalling the fun times they had with them and laughing about the stupid stuff we've all done together. I sit there and listen. I'm not ready to talk about them yet. I can't talk about them like they're gone. It starts to get dark, and everyone starts to leave, but I'm not ready yet.

Tyler crouches down in front of me, like he's protecting me from the world. "Are you coming, Addie?"

"Not yet, I just want to sit here a little while longer. I'd like to be alone with her for a bit, if that's okay?"

He nods even though I can tell he's not happy about leaving me.

"I'll be okay, I promise. I'll come and find you later?" I whisper.

He stands and walks back towards the dorms.

Once he's gone, the silence hits me. I pick up the picture of us and hug it to my chest. I push backwards and lean against the tree, closing my eyes. It's almost like she's still here. The wind starts to whip through the trees and I listen to the leaves rustling – the sounds of life going on in the distance. It's almost like I can feel her here with me, sat quietly with me, like we used to. I pull my knees up to my chest and wrap my arms around myself as I cry.

Someone sits down beside me and I guess that Ty wasn't prepared to leave me alone after all. My sobs have taken over my body and all I can do is hold on to myself. I'm pulled sideways into a hug, and I land on a wall of muscle. I immediately know it is not Ty. I look up to see Xander holding me. His arms are lock around me like a vice.

"You'll be okay, Addie. Let it out. I know it hurts now, but she'll always be here with you," he soothes. "I've got you."

I cry until I can't cry anymore. He hasn't moved since he sat with me; I don't know how long we've been sat like this, but I feel like stone.

"Thank you, Xander. I'm sorry."

"Never be sorry for feeling, Addie." He tucks my hair away from my face. "Are you going to be okay?" he asks.

He's so close that I can feel his breath on my face. Something alien stirs in the pit of my stomach. My emotions are everywhere.

"I will be. Thank you, again." I stumble over the words. We're so close, and I feel so comfortable here with him. I shake my head, trying to dislodge the confusion. I go to stand and he beats me to it, his Vampyr reflexes mean he moves quickly. He holds out a hand to help me. I take it and once up, smooth down my trousers and blouse, suddenly very aware of how much of a mess I must look.

"I'm just going to head back to my dorm, I didn't realise how late it got," I say.

It's got dark whilst we sat, but the moon is shining so brightly it reflects off him, making him almost luminescent. I take a moment to look at him; I've never seen him like this before. His shirt is slightly undone and his hair is ruffled. He looks unguarded, and it makes my stomach flip in a way I don't understand. It's almost like seeing him naked. I feel the blush creep up my cheeks.

He nods, almost as if he's dismissing me, and I turn and leave. I dare to turn back, and he's still stood in the same spot, watching me as I walk away.

XANDER

I see her sat there up against the tree, curled into herself, and it kills me that she's as broken as she is. This is my fault. I should have been there; I should have protected her better. My skin feels like it's on fire with the vengeance I want to reap on Kaden. I can't help but feel he planned it so I would be far away - knowing I would never make it back in time. It's crazy, but I know him. He's an arsehole, and after the last time we met, it's about right that he would try to hit me where it hurts. He knows how much the humans and this Academy, mean to me.

The urge to go and comfort her is overwhelming, but I know it is not my place. I feel regret burn through my veins; her tears are worse than any punishment that could be bestowed upon me. Each tear feels like a whip tearing open the skin on my back. *Fuck it!* I can't just stand here and watch as she drowns in herself. I almost run to her side, and she doesn't even notice my approach. She seems so young in this moment. She has no idea of what is to come, of the pain she is destined to endure – and I want to wrap her up and protect her from all of it.

I sit beside her and wrap her up in my arms. She fits so perfectly against me, and I feel that same jolt I felt the first time I held her. But she is forbidden, and nothing will make me break my vow.

DESCENT

"You'll be okay, Addie, let it out. I know it hurts now, but she'll always be here with you," I whisper into her hair. "I've got you." *If only she knew.*

She sobs into my arms and I can feel the pain radiating from her. I do the only thing I can think of. I weave my mind to her, and I can feel all her emotions; her pain, her guilt. The burden she carries for her lost friend is crippling. It's clouding her light. The small beams of her light fight the shadows surrounding her soul but the shadows threaten to extinguish the good inside her.

The darker side of her is encouraging the shadows to take hold, whispering to her, letting her believe the pain is the best way to survive. I grasp onto the strands of the shadow and suck some of it into myself. Not too much, but enough to help her breathe. If anyone knew what I had done, that I had shown part of my true self to her, the punishment would be unthinkable – but I cannot let her be taken over by that other part of her. *She would lose herself,* I reason, knowing it wouldn't matter. Too many secrets, too many lives are at stake. I feel her tears stop, the shadows I absorbed finally allowing her to breathe.

"Thank you, Xander. I'm sorry," she says.

Her hair blows across her face in the wind. *Mesmerising.*

"Never be sorry for feeling, Addie. Are you going to be okay?" I ask, relishing how close she is to me.

"I will be." She tries to stand and stumbles. I reach out to stop her falling. I can sense her embarrassment.

"I'm going to head back; I didn't realise how late it got."

"If you ever need me, I'm here for you."

She nods, casting me the most unfathomable look, and then leaves me. I watch as she walks away, waiting until she is out of sight before making my way back to my own quarters. I walk slowly, enjoying the cold air on my skin.

"Xander?" I turn and see Aliana, one of my Elite team.

"Yes, Aliana?" I ask with concern; it's rare for her to leave the administration building.

"They will be here at dawn tomorrow, we've made space for them as requested, and only myself and Dimitri are aware of their arrival."

"Very well. Thank you, Aliana. I'll be down to meet them in the morning."

ADDIE

"Addie! Save me! Don't let them take me away!" Livvy screams as three Shades drag her down the hall in front of me. I try to move but it's like there are lead weights on my feet. I struggle to chase after her.

"Addie!"

DESCENT

"I'm coming, Livvy!" I struggle free and run down the hall after her. That's when I the door to the Defence room isn't there anymore, and Livvy is on the floor, broken and bleeding. I rush to her and trip over my feet. Then I hear Kaden laughing.

"Looks like you failed, Adelaide. You're such a disappointment; you had the power to save her, but you didn't use it. You failed. Now you get to watch and remember. This is all your fault." He taunts me from the shadows. I try to get up from the floor, but pain radiates through my body as if I've broken every bone. Then I see my Sai on her throat.

There's so much blood.

"You didn't save me, Addie," Livvy cries. "Why didn't you save me? Why didn't you keep your promise?"

I scream as I shoot upright in bed. My hair is matted to my face, and I can feel the layer of cold sweat covering my body as I sit and shake. *It was just a dream.* I look around and note that I'm alone. Tyler didn't stay here last night. A wave of panic washes over me. He's stayed with me every night since it happened, sleeping on the sofa, and I'm not sure how to feel about the fact he's not here now. I look over to the clock and see it's only five in the morning. I know I'm never getting back to sleep, so decide to get a shower and get ready for the day.

As I stand under the scalding hot water, I can't help but see her lifeless face in my memory. I can still hear her crying out to me. I wrap my arms around myself, knowing she is going to haunt me for the rest of my life. It's then I resolve to work even harder to join the Red Guard. I never want to feel like that again.

I pull myself together and put on my jumpsuit for Defence. I get my stuff together to head out for a run before class. Just as I head for the door, there's a knock on it before it swings open to show a pissed off looking Ty.

"What's up with you?" I ask. I've not seen him this angry since he lost a sparring match with Noah – he hates him as much as I do.

"I'm surprised you noticed. You didn't notice me when you were cuddled up to that Vampyr! What's wrong Addie? Human's not good enough for you? You want to be with one of *them.* He's no different from the filth that killed Livvy and Logan," he spits out.

"I have no idea what you're talking about Tyler. So why don't you chill your shit and actually talk to me like I'm your girlfriend; if that's even what I am?

I have no idea what his problem is, but I can't deal with his shit as well as my own.

"I came back outside last night," he says, running his hands through his hair, "to make sure you were okay, and you were all wrapped up in Xander-fucking-Bane. That's what the hell is 'up', Addie. I didn't figure you for a Fanger."

DESCENT

"What the actual fuck, Tyler! I was on my own, crying my eyes out and he came over to make sure I was okay. Fuck you and fuck your stupid standards! Get the hell out of my way."

I put on Livvy's headphones and start the music, pushing past Ty and sprinting out of the dorm. I don't pay attention to where I'm running until I'm in the middle of a field, bent over catching my breath. That's when I see the Elite are at the Academy. Why would they arrive this early? And why has no one said that they're coming? Xander and Dimitri are speaking to them and I'm not sure if they've seen me – but they're freaking Vampyrs so of course they know I'm here. The Elite are dismissed and file into the staff quarters of The Academy. I turn and stretch out, ready to head to Defence class when suddenly,

"Morning Adelaide. Enjoying your run?" Xander Bane stands in front of me as casually as if he didn't just totally vamp out on me and super speed over here in the blink of an eye.

"It was just what I needed, thank you. Did you want something? Or can I get on my way to Defence?"

"You can't let anyone know they're here," he says sternly.

"The Elite?"

"Yes, we have reason to believe another attack is coming, and having them here gives us an advantage;

especially if no one knows they're here. Do you understand?"

"Strategically, yes I understand. But if you think there's going to be another attack, why aren't you warning people? Making sure they're prepared?"

"And what if by doing that, we let the enemy know what's going on? What's to say someone in here isn't working with them? Their attack was planned, as if they knew exactly where people would be, when the guard would be most vulnerable and where."

"Are you saying someone helped those monsters?" I ask, my head spinning with potential suspects.

"I'm not saying anything, just, keep this to yourself. Please."

"Fine, but if more people die because they weren't prepared, that's on you. Just remember that."

"I'm fully aware of my fault in all of this. I am responsible for the safety of The Academy at all times. I failed, and I'm trying to make sure that doesn't happen again."

"Fine," I say begrudgingly. I'm sure he has a good reason; he certainly thinks he does.

"Do you run every day?" he asks.

"Yes, every morning," I say, confused as to why he'd ask.

"Maybe I'll join you; I need to get some more cardio in," he winks.

DESCENT

"Ermmm…" I stammer. I have no idea what do say to him.

"I'll see you in class, Miss Tate."

"Sorry, what?" I ask confused, but I'm talking to air. He's gone. *Stupid Vampyr tricks.*

I head to Defence, knowing what I need today is just to zone out and work my body hard. If my body is tired, I won't be able to think.

Dimitri puts us through our paces in warm up, the cardio workout has me sweating so badly that it drips off of my face and down my neck.

"Right, guys, everyone is going to be doing some one on one sparring. Xander Bane is going to be joining us and every Defence class, to help with defence against the Shades," Dimitri announces. A groan rolls out across the room. Dimitri works us hard enough on his own – just great!

"What good is he going to be to us? He's a washed up house leader. He's no warrior," Tyler snarls.

My jaw slacks – I can't believe Ty would say something so out of line. I'm guess he's still got a bug up his ass.

"Well, Mr. Knight, I'm sure you're aware from your study of the Dark War, Xander was a major reason our side won. Maybe, instead of mouthing off, you should be working harder."

"Maybe he was the big time back in the war, but since then, he's been less than great. First, the princess died on his watch. Then there was the attack here. He's meant to be the one keeping us safe. He obviously can't do that, so I don't see what we'll learn from him."

I watch Ty's complete car-crash of self-destruction and my stomach flips when I hear Xander from the doorway.

"Well, I guess, Mr Knight, you won't have any problem sparring with me today then?" He's staring Tyler down, and the testosterone in this room is off the chart. It's so quiet you could hear a pin drop. "Unless you're afraid that a wash out like me could beat you?"

Tyler's face goes so red I think he might burst and his humiliation is firing his aggression. "Ha! You're on old man."

Him and his stupid big mouth. He's got too much pride to just take it back. Idiot.

Xander walks in, shrugging off his leather jacket and boots, placing them neatly by the wall. Then walks barefoot, to meet Tyler in the middle of the room. Everyone else has moved to the edges of the room, forming a circle around them. I don't know if I even want to watch this. They start to spar, and with every missed hit, I can see Ty getting more and more worked up. But Xander is stealthy and sleek, like a big cat. He keeps his cool, trying to wear Tyler out before he goes in for the kill. This

113

is not going to be pretty. Normally, I'd place my bets on Tyler, but there's a reason Xander is the Head of his house. He worked his way up, and I can only hazard a guess at what it takes to *stay* the Head of a Vampyr house.

The fight was brutal, and Ty ended up getting his ass kicked even though he gave it everything he had. Every ounce of hatred he held for Xander was on his face, in his every move. He wasn't holding back, not even a little, yet Xander swatted him like he was nothing more than a fly. It was hard to watch.

Ty stormed off afterwards to clean his wounds and stroke his ego. Humiliation doesn't even cover what just happened to him – he was destroyed.

Everyone filters out of the room at the end of class, leaving me alone with Dimitri and Xander.

"Did you really have to go at him so hard?" I ask.

"Would you rather I took it easy on him? Let him think he could beat me so he doesn't bother to try and better himself? What I did was for his own good."

"Maybe, but you didn't have to enjoy it so much."

"She has a point, Xander. You pummelled him into the ground, and you smiled whilst you did it," Dimitri pipes up.

Xander smiles smugly and shrugs his shoulders before turning to the door, picking up his boots and jacket on the way. He turns to face us, the smile still on his face. "Fanger haters should be put in their place. Don't you agree, Adelaide?"

Xander Bane is the last thing that should be on my mind, but I can't help myself. Even with everything else going on around me, I know there is something going on between us, something that wasn't there before. Sure, he's good looking, but I've never thought about him like *that* before, not really. I shake my head and rid my thoughts of him. Now is not the time for me to get a crush on a Vampyr. I have so much else to deal with right now that I don't need to add to it.

XANDER

I stretch out on the green, looking forward to my morning run; knowing I'll get to spend time with her again. We've run like every morning since The Elite arrived, and even though I know I'm pushing the boundaries of what I should and shouldn't do, I can't bring myself to stop.

All we do is run, we occasionally talk, but more often than not, we just enjoy the comfortable silence of each other's company. Since she lost her friends, she's crying out for someone to depend on, someone to be there for her, and that dickweed Tyler obviously isn't doing that.

The rage, which bubbles up just thinking about him, is overwhelming. There is something off about him. I can't put my finger on what it is but I just don't like him. And I refuse to believe it's down to jealousy like Dimitri says. Either way, I'm keeping an eye on him.

I see her coming, having already started her run from her dorm round to the front gate, and I can't help but be taken away by her. Her beauty is undeniable. The jumpsuit hugs her every curve, making my mouth water. I can't help the direction my thoughts take as I watch her swaying her hips as she slows when she gets closer.

"Good morning, Adelaide," I say. "I'm impressed by your dedication. Are you ready?"

"Please, I've already done three laps this morning. Are you ready, old man?"

I can't help the bark of laughter that escapes me.

"Old man? I barely look twenty-five. Anyway, isn't it true you're as young as you feel? I could still run rings around you."

"Ha! You could try. I'm sure that stamina of yours would fizz out," she smirks. Her flirty manner has become more obvious the past few days as she's become more comfortable around me, and I'm not going to deny enjoying it.

"My stamina knows no bounds, Miss Tate." I wink at her and take off at a speed I know she can catch up to. I have to remember she's only human. Holding back is nothing I'm not used to, having been around humans for as long as I have; but I find myself wanting to show her everything. Who I really am. The wonders this world holds. I want to give her everything, and never let hurt touch her again. I want to protect her from the evil I know this world holds. For now, I will settle for this. For her friendship: for her trust

"Come on, slow poke!" I call back to her. "I thought you had this."

"Yeah, yeah, old man. I was taking it easy on you, letting you think you had the lead," she laughs. "What's the fun in beating you when you can see it coming?" And with that, she pushes herself harder to take the lead. I let her keep her lead for a while, before joining her pace and running side by side with her.

I hear the bell ring in the distance, the advantage of being what I am.

"Time to go, Addie. Same time tomorrow?"

"You can count on it," she says, before starting towards the main building. She turns and waves back to me halfway and she catches me watching her. What can I say? I'm a guy, and her arse in that suit deserves watching.

DESCENT

Chapter Seven

ADDIE

I stand on the mats and roll my shoulders. Defence class is the one class I've not needed to worry about. I've been the top of my class for years. Yes, I've only fought other humans, who in reality are no match for Demons or Vampyrs, but I've got this test.

Dimitri steps onto the mat. Oh hell no! Our test is fighting him? I'm so screwed. I groan internally and clench my teeth. That mothertrucker is going to enjoy this. His goofy smile is a disguise; I know he's going to knock me on my ass as soon as he gets a chance. It's then I realise there's more Vampyrs in here than just Dimitri – the Heads of all eight Vampyr houses sit at the head table, watching my every move.

Breath, Addie, you can do this. Just focus and remember your training. Do not let him stay on the attack,

119

otherwise you'll tire. Let your size work for you, no one thinks a five foot three human is a match for a Vampyr. I lock eyes with Xander and I see the smirk that graces his face. Dick. He's seen me fight but he's looking forward to seeing me get beat; it's written all over that pretty English face of his.

I take another deep breath and take a step forward. Dimitri meets my eyes and his face changes, he becomes the warrior I know he is, and I watch his entire body transform. He nods, showing the Heads that he is ready. I nod, too and hope to God he doesn't kick my ass.

Ugh. He totally kicked my ass! Now, I'm a sweaty, exhausted mess. I was so happy about landing a few hits in the beginning that I got lazy. And I know it. Dammit! At least I pinned him and he didn't get a kill shot. I want out of this hell hole, and passing this class is a must to get out. I hate the evaluation stage. So many tests, to see which place in society fits you best. No choice about what I want to do. What they tell me I'm doing is what I'll spend the rest of my life doing. I hate it. It's the only reason I've worked so hard; I refuse to be someone at the bottom of the ladder. I was not meant to be someone's maid, plus, have you seen my room? Tidy isn't exactly my strong suit.

I grab a bottle of water from the table and stand at the back of the room, sneaking a peek at the Heads of houses. Sure I've seen The Eight here before, they're here every year at the evaluations, but I've never had chance to watch them closely. They sit, so human like, and yet they seem like statues, too. For beings that can move so fast, they can be eerily still.

Xander Bane might just be the hottest Vampyr I've ever seen, but he's also a total dick. I don't get why he thinks he's so much better than everyone else. I mean, everyone knows the Valoire Princess died whilst his house was on watch. Who knows, maybe that's why he's such a dick – maybe the guilt eats at him. Still no excuse though. Dammit, why does he have to be so pretty? I stand at the back of the room, studying the frown lines on his face, when he spots me checking him out. Fuck! It's not like I can just look away! And now he's just watching as I stand here and gawp at him. I need to look away. Any time now would be good. Why am I still looking at him! I see the edges of his mouth turn up as he watches me. For the love of all that's holy! I bite my lip praying to whatever forces there are for this to stop. I can feel the heat in my face. I'm with Tyler for crying out loud. Some stupid, whiplash-worthy mood swinging Vampyr shouldn't have this effect on me!

DESCENT

The bell rings to announce the end of the latest evaluation, and I manage to tear my eyes away from him. Thank Fuck! Poor Benny though, looks like he took a beating; he's bruised and bloody, as Dimitri offers him a hand up from the mats.

Dimitri works through the class, some doing okay, others not so much. I almost cheered out loud when he knocked Noah out after a few minutes, even if they were an intense few minutes!

We were asked to wait outside whilst the Eight deliberated, and I can't help my nervous excitement. Right now is where I'll find out if I made it. Dimitri is out here with us, trying to keep us all in line as we wait to be called back in.

The door opens and we all file in. They call us up each by name, alphabetically by surname, telling us if we passed the Eval, and if we'd like to be part of the guard if we passed. They then approve or deny the request. I'm so excited! Ty has already been approved, and I totally failed at holding in my squeal of happiness for him, now we can both be together in the guard, too. Noah is called forward and I snigger to myself. After that performance, there is no way he can get in the guard. He steps forward and is addressed by Xander.

"Noah Remington, you have passed your evaluation. Well done. Is it your wish to join the Red Guard should you graduate the Academy?" he asks.

"Sir. Yes Sir, it would be an honour." Noah recites the standard answer. Xander looks at him, scrutinising him inch by inch.

"Approved."

My jaw hits the floor. No. Freaking. Way! I can't believe he was approved! They must be in real need of people for the guard if he got through after that. I look at Dimitri, who's shock mirrors my own. Noah walks back to the back of the room and smirks at me. Freaking ejit.

"Adelaide Tate," Xander calls my name and I momentarily freeze. This is it! I look to Dimitri, who nods in encouragement, a small smile on his face. I walk over and stand to attention, as is required.

"Adelaide Tate, you have passed your evaluation. Well done. Is it your wish to join the Red Guard should you graduate the Academy?" he asks me, the same as he has done to everyone else. I'm so excited right now I could bounce.

"Sir. Yes, Sir, it would be an honour," I shout.

He examines me, and while I'm sure it only lasts a minute, it feels like forever. Then I hear him speak, and it's as if I'm inside a bubble. I can hear Dimitri shouting but it's muffled

"Denied."

What? I replay his words in my mind. I'm frozen to the spot. The world is spinning. *"Denied. Your request has not been approved."*

123

DESCENT

"What?"

"You are dismissed, Miss Tate."

I walk to the back of the room in a daze, unable to process what just happened. Dimitri is still shouting, but I can't register what he's saying.

Ty is stood against the wall behind me, his arms crossed. He looks pissed, but not as pissed as I'm going to be, I'm sure. I will not let them see how much they just broke me. I walk over to him, grab his hand and drag him out of the room.

"Addie!" I hear my name shouted from behind me, but I can't stop. If I stop now, I'll break, and I can't do that, not after everything, so pick up our pace. I drop Ty's hand and take off at a run, back to my room. I fall to the floor as the tears descend. Ty finds me, gathering me in his arms.

"I am so sorry, baby girl. For everything. We'll fix this." He picks me up in his arms and I bury my face in his neck. Everything about him brings me comfort. The feel of him wrapped around me, his smell so earthy. I wish that just for a few seconds, I could lose myself in it all and stop caring about everything else. He walks me over to my bed and lays us down on it. I'm totally entwined in him. I open my eyes to look at him and he's staring down at me, stroking my hair, but my eyes wander, there's something wrong. The room on Livvy's side is completely empty. The dam shatters and I can't hold it back anymore. They've tried to erase her. All of Livvy's things are gone – even her bed. There's just a small pile at the edge of my bed. They're really gone, and now the Guard is gone, too.

I've never felt so helpless and so useless. It's not a surprise I didn't get in The Guard. They're gone because of me. I cry on Tyler's shoulder, crying so hard, I can't catch my breath. I'm so tired, I can barely keep my eyes open.

"It's okay, baby girl, just sleep. I'll be here when you wake up. Right here," he whispers into my hair and kissing my forehead.

"I love you, Ty," I whisper before darkness wraps its way around me.

When I wake, the room is shrouded in darkness, and Ty is still next to me. I'm lying in the comfort of his arms, my eyes closing again when the memory hits me. My eyes fly open; I'm definitely awake now. Holy shit! I did *not* say *that* before I went to sleep, right?

I love you, Ty.

I squeeze my eyes tight hoping and wishing it was all just a bad dream, but I know it wasn't. God damn it! Why would I say something so stupid? It's not even true…

Is it? Quietly panicking, I know that if I try to move, he'll wake up, and I *really* don't want that!

"Addie, please stop thinking so loud," Ty grumbles half asleep, and I can't help but giggle. Oops.

"I think I'm going to go for a run," I say. He responds by hugging me tighter.

"Not now, Addie, I don't want to be alone. I need you here," he murmurs to me, and I let out a deep breath. "I need you here. Please."

"I'm not going anywhere," I say kissing him and snuggling back down onto his chest. I can't leave him now. He releases a breath and it occurs to me he's struggling as much as I am; he's just holding it all together for me. I'm so thankful he's still here, and that he's mine.

"I love you, Addie. Forever and always," he says just before his breathing evens out, and he falls back to sleep.

Today has been one of the worst days of my life, probably number three on the scale, but this, this makes it all seem like a test to see if I was worthy of someone like him in my life.

Xander

Dimitri follows me to my office and I can feel the anger rolling from him. In all our years as friends, I've never seen him so invested, and so worked up over a girl.

"Xander, what the fuck are you thinking?! That girl is the best damn fighter I've seen in a long time, and considering how old I am, that says a fucking lot! She could be the best warrior of her kind. Hell, she could be better than some of ours!" he yells as soon as the door closes.

I sigh as I drop into the leather chair seated behind my imposing mahogany desk.

"You don't understand, Dimitri, there's so much you don't know; About her, about everything – and I can't explain properly. You just need to trust me when I say she can't be part of The Guard."

"I trust you, but you've got to give me something here, man. She pinned you in practice. I can't remember the last person, man or beast who managed to do that. There's just something about her, you know? I feel like she's my little sister, and I want her to have everything she ever wanted. The look on her face when you rejected her, it damn near tore my heart out."

I run my hand through my hair, whilst desperately hoping he lets this go. That practice where she pinned me was like pure and utter torture. I didn't want to hurt her, but I couldn't hold back. I hadn't with anyone else, but the bloody vixen caught me out. She is so fucking talented, her movements so swift and graceful, she's like an avenging angel. I was distracted by her tongue poking out of her lips, she does it when she's focusing, and I couldn't help but think about it and all of the wondrous things… and then she bloody pinned me. She was on top of me, straddling me, panting, her hair in my face. Fucking. Torture. Keeping myself in check with her on top of me like that was not the easiest thing to do. I smirk before answering him.

"Oh, I know, Dimitri, believe me, I know." He couldn't even begin to understand the hold she has over me, and while I try to fight it every damn day, I know that soon, it's probably going to win.

"If you think I didn't die a little inside, then you're wrong. I felt her heart break. Then I saw the emptiness take over, and I know you've seen it, too; that other side of her. That's part of why she can't join The Guard. What we are, it affects her too much. What *they* are affects her, too. I know I sound like a cryptic son of a bitch, but you know I wouldn't keep it from you if it wasn't what's best for her." I can almost see his brain ticking away, trying to piece it all together. Maybe he'll work it out on his own, and then I'll finally have someone I can speak to about it all, but until then, the secret is mine to burden. He nods at me, and turns to leave. He stops at the door and looks back at me.

"You know, you can't stop whatever path she's on, Xander, and from the sounds of it, she needs all the help she can get. It's bad enough they're not told the truth in their classes, but if you're keeping something from her that could change who she fundamentally is, then she needs to know sooner rather than later." He finishes and leaves, closing the door behind him. *Shit.* This is turning into an absolute shit storm. I hate that I've been put in this position. Seventeen years ago, I agreed to help with a plan, and while I would have never made a different choice, I sometimes wish one of my brothers had been the one to make the oath I made.

"Please, Xander, I have no one else to turn to. She is an innocent life in this never-ending war. Kellen doesn't understand, he cannot be reasonable in this decision. His anger would cloud his judgement." She begs me as she clings to my arm.

I look down at her, a woman begging to save the life of her child, there is no possible way I can turn her away. The bundle wrapped up in her arms looks up at me, and I feel as if she can see my soul, what is left of it. I feel the pang in my heart and know that this decision will affect many things to come; the weight of this will ripple through the coming years with no idea of the repercussions.

"Are you sure of this, Lan? Defying him could be the end of you. The end of me. Of us all. If he ever found out – I dare not think of the consequences."

DESCENT

"I've never been more sure of anything in my entire existence. I have been alive a long, long time, Xander. She was created for a reason, even if we do not know that reason right now, even if I have no memory of it. It is not her fault. I can feel her, Xander; she was born for greatness. I cannot kill her just because he might decree it, or because the council do. He wouldn't understand, which is how I can be safe in my choice. All he knows is that we have a daughter, if he found out the truth… I can't fathom his reaction."

She says it with such conviction, that even if I hadn't made a decision, I would be swayed to her will. I can see the fire in her eyes, the determination to save her daughter. I will take the child to the Nursery. They will care for her as a human, that is all they will know her as.

"I have hidden her from this world, she has been cloaked by my magic. She, nor anyone else around her will ever know who, or what she is. Her appearance will be changed so that she is not recognised. This is the only way I can think of to keep her safe – until the time comes that she needs to be exactly who she is." She kisses her daughters head and I see her magic take hold. The child's features will change significantly, so no-one will ever know what she is. She hands the child to me with a tear running down her cheek.

"Goodbye, Aeveen, my beautiful light. I will see you again, daughter. In this life or the next," she says to her

daughter before looking up at me. "Make the oath to me,
Xander. Swear you will make sure she is always cared for.
That she is always safe.

"I swear to you, Lan. I will put my life in service of
hers." I nod and walk away with the child smiling up at me.
I can't help but smile back at her.

"You need a new name, beautiful light," I say to her,
and she coos back at me.

That's when I first knew that she had stolen a part of
me. I've tried to distance myself as much as I can from her
so she can experience the life she deserves, before her
other life is thrust upon her. But to allow her in The Guard,
would be putting her in the very danger I vowed to keep
her from.

She needs to learn the truth about herself, the truth
about our world rather than the 'truth' she has been
taught. The need to do what is best for her, battles against
the vow I made inside me. She has already been exposed
to them, and I fear Kaden's true reason for entering the
school. It has been many years since he faced me, and I
thought that last time would truly be the last. My
vengeance had not been swift, but it was exacted. If he

knows the truth, then that means that… No, I can't think like that. I need to think it was merely a coincidence that they toyed with her. It's not possible they know. Is it?

ADDIE

"Come on, Addie, let me get you out of here. We deserve a few hours of just us," Tyler says from the table behind me.

"Tyler, can we just get through this Eval first, and then I'll let you know? You know how much I suck at History of the Races, and after the mess I made in Home Ec..."

I cringe thinking about the oven I managed to blow up. So what if I left the gas on a little longer than I should've before igniting it. It's not my fault Stacy now has no eyebrows! It's also not my fault I managed to either burn or undercook everything I made for the Eval. Home skills are so not my thing.

"I *need* to do well on this one. Especially since there's no chance of The Red Guard for me now." I sigh. Yes, I'm still sore about it. Considering they let Noah in, I have no idea why I didn't get in, and I'm yet to get a decent answer from either of those bloody Vampyrs. Telling me it's for my own good, for my own safety is a big ol' steaming pile of crap. I deserve that spot. I worked my whole life for that spot. And they gave it to that jerk-off. Someone, somewhere, is making real great decisions.

"That's exactly why we need this, Addie. You need to just relax, let some of it go. I'm not telling you to calm down, believe me, I'm not making that mistake again. My jaw still aches from last time," he rubs his jaw, laughing quietly. "I just mean; it'll be good for both of us to have some time, just us. Away from people. Human, Vampyr, Fae. All of them. I kinda miss you, Ads. It feels ages since we just hung out."

What's a girl to say to that? I mean, really?! I turn around to face him, all big eyes and floppy hair. I'm trying not to pay attention to the bulging biceps, and to forget about the yummy abs, because then I'll forget that I was going to say.... Wait. Nope, it's gone. I look back into his eyes, and remember he asked me a question.

"Okay, okay. We can hang out, just us. What did you have in mind?"

"Well… I was thinking a picnic out in that clearing in the forest. You know where I mean?"

"Yeah, I know the spot, the wildflowers there are so pretty."

"Yeah, that's the one. And you know, clothing *is* optional." He wags his eyebrows and I burst out laughing.

What an idiot. I slap his arm playfully so he knows I didn't mean to laugh quite so much.

"Uh-huh. Optional means I'm wearing them. You however, you can go topless." I wink at him and turn back to my desk, as the Keeper who teaches this class walks in. The buzzer sounds to start class and I feel a prod in my back.

"Ha, I'm totally going to rock your world," I hear Ty whisper over my shoulder.

The Keeper hands out the test for the Eval, and I can feel the cold sweat already. I hate tests. Give me a battle any day.

"You have three hours to complete the test in full. This test makes up one hundred percent of your result. Good Luck," she announces. Other than the occasional tap of a pencil on a desk, it's so quiet.

Gah, I need to focus! The clock ticks and it's driving me nuts. *Come on, Addie, you can do this.* I look down at the paper and the first question makes me want to bang my head on my desk. Why do I need to know the names of all of the Fae Royals from the Dark War, and their roles in the war? Or the Vampyrs? Gah! I hate this stuff!

I knuckle down and work through the paper. By the time the buzzer signals time is up, my hand is cramping and I'm scribbling down my final answers. I lift my head and see the Keeper walking towards me to collect my paper. Ty wraps his arms around my waist and lifts me up onto his knee. I try so hard not to squeak, but I freaking hate being picked up. Even if it is kind of sweet.

"Mr Knight, I didn't realise your ambition in life was to be a stool for Miss Tate."

"Well you see, Miss, Addie here is kind of delicate, and she's been sat on your hard stool for three hours." He says playfully, "I figured I'd give her cute ass a cushion," he smirks. The sound of stifled laughter echoes around the room. I can even see the Keeper try not to smile at Ty. His charm has no bounds, it emanates from him and drags you in, and once you're in, that's it. You're a goner, there is no escape.

"Well, Mr Knight, that's all well and good, but I'm sure Miss Tate will survive a few more moments without you, as this is officially the end of your last History of the Races class – as long as you pass, of course," she smirks back at him.

"Now then, you rotten lot, be gone. I don't want to see your faces in here again, so you better have done well. Go and enjoy your weekend!" The room erupts with sound and movement as people start gathering their things and leaving, happy to escape into the sunshine. I grab my bag and wait for Tyler to get his stuff. He hooks his arm around my waist and we make our way out of the room, and out of the building.

The sunshine feels beautiful on my skin; it's been a while since I've let myself enjoy the little things, but I know how angry Livvy would be if she could see how sad I've been. The last few days have gone by in a whirlwind. I've not spent a night away from Ty since the attack, and now he's even more attentive than he was before. I've managed to avoid Dimitri and Xander for the most part, too. I'm trying not to focus on the negatives, but now I have no idea exactly what I'm going to do with myself. I feel a bad because Ty hasn't really celebrated the fact he's now part of The Guard, along with Benny and the guys, and I know it's because of me.

We're sat out on the green by the forest, in our spot for Livvy and Logan, lying in the sun, just being, when a shadow eclipses the bright light beating down on my eyelids.

"Come on, love birds, you've had enough time alone for now." Opening my eyes, I see Benny looming above me and I roll my eyes at him.

"You're going to regret that, Short Stack!" he says before he leans down and picks me up. He tickles me until I squeal for mercy and then drops down to the floor with me still over his shoulder, before pulling me down so I'm sat in his lap.

"I don't think your angry warrior is all that happy about your positioning, Miss Tate. I wonder what he'd do if I..." he finishes his question by grabbing my face and kissing me to push Tyler's buttons. It's just a quick kiss, and it's over before it starts. He pulls back and laughs a deep belly laugh at Ty who is now standing and growling at him, looking like he's going to explode.

"You're going to regret that, Benny boy," he barks out while clenching his fists at his sides.

"It's okay, Ty, he was just goofing off, trying to wind you up. Calm down," I say, trying to defuse the situation a little, I'm not exactly okay with it, but I don't want these guys facing off over it either. I can see the veins in Ty's forearms bulge, as he builds himself up. Benny lifts me by the waist and plonks me on the ground next to where he's sat. As soon as I'm clear, Ty is running at him and I hear the whoosh of breath as he hits Benny. They end up rolling around on the floor blowing off steam, until it ends in them both laughing as they separate. Boys! They get up of the floor and hug it out in that weird boyish way that they do, and swagger back over to where I'm sat.

"All better?" I ask sarcastically. They both just grunt at me as they sit back on the floor, Ty sitting behind me and pulling me on his lap. Stupid territorial caveman.

"You going to pee on me next Ty? I mean really!" I push up off of his lap and sit back down on my own. "I am not your trophy to be won, to be shown off like a damn prize. Now swallow your stupid pride and handle your ego," I snap at him. It's only funny for a little while.

I can hear Benny sniggering and I snap my eyes up to him. "Really, Benny? You want some, too?"

"Oh, I had mine already babe." He laughs and I roll my eyes again, before punching him solidly in jaw.

"Enough, Benny!" I scold him, once I can let slide, but twice is too much.

"Ouch!" he yells, rubbing his jaw. "I deserved that, so I'll take it. Anyway, the whole reason I came to find you guys is because I decided we need to celebrate! Our Evals are finally done. All that's left is placements and we already know where we're heading."

I must visibly cringe because Benny's face flickers with guilt and Ty takes my hand in his. "Sorry Addie, I forgot. You know I'm an idiot."

"It's fine, Benny," I say with a fake smile, "I don't want you guys not to celebrate. You finally did it! What we've all worked for what seems like forever for. Of course you need to celebrate."

"Okay, well the idea is a mini prom. So that you know, we didn't spend all that money for just one night. So all the guys are busting out their suits, and the girls are putting on their dresses. You guys will be there right? Nine tonight at mine?"

"Sure thing," Ty says casually, squeezing my hand tighter. I look over to the clock tower and notice it's nearly five already, so we head back and grab some food from the mess hall.

"I need to go do something," Ty says to me as he stands up and kisses me. "I won't be long, are you going to be okay here?" he asks and I nod. Benny doesn't mean any harm, and I can more than handle him.

"If you're sure," he says, eyeing Benny. "I'll come grab you before we head over to Benny's okay?"

I nod, confused at his vagueness. This has happened a few times recently, but I've put it down to being stuff for The Guard that he didn't want to tell me about. I don't question him though; I don't want to be that girl. So I watch him leave before I gather my things and head back up to my room.

I keep forgetting how bare this room feels now that they took away almost every trace of Livvy. I sit on my bed and see my cluttered half of the room and decide enough is enough. I shrug off my jacket and put my hair up. I might not have long left in this room, but for now, it's mine and I'm going to make it feel that way. I start moving the remaining furniture around, until the room looks less like it's missing its other half. I've put the pictures of us up on the walls, all except the one of the four of us at prom. That's in its frame on my bedside table. I look around and I swear I can feel Livvy here giving me her approval. Tears spring to my eyes.

"I miss you, Livvy. I have no idea what I'm going to do without you."

I grab my shower stuff, making a start on getting ready for tonight – not that I want to go. I try not to think too much about how the hell I'm going to manage my hair and makeup myself, or where the hell Ty has gone, and just concentrate on getting through tonight. It's going to be a hard task to keep my happy face on all night. I take a deep breath, pull up my big girl pants, and deal. I refuse to be the reason my friends hide their success. Will this totally suck for me? Hell, yes it will, but I am not selfish enough to deny them their happiness.

After my shower, I slip my dress on and think back to the last time I wore it. There's a knock at my door and I assume it's Ty.

"Come in!" I yell, pulling the dress up over my hips.

"Errrr, sorry, Addie, I didn't realise…" Benny splutters.

I hurriedly finish putting on my dress, trying not to laugh too much.

"It's okay Benny, what's up?" I say casting a look over my shoulder to see Benny turned to the wall and squirming. I laugh a little, "You can turn back around, I'm not naked."

He turns around and is the colour of a beet. Who would've thought!

"Erm… right, yeah. Ty popped by a little while ago and asked me to come and bring you over to the party because he's going to be a little late. I'm going to go ahead and guess he didn't tell you?"

"That would be a no. Never mind, I guess."

We head over to Benny's dorm room, and I can hear the music before we even enter the building.

DESCENT

"I wonder how long until this one gets shut down," I say, nudging his arm with my shoulder.

"Don't you worry your pretty little head about that one, darlin', I told big D about this one and he said he'd help us out." He winks at me.

"You mean Dimitri? Seriously?" The shock must be evident on my face because he bursts out laughing.

"Yeah, Addie, he's not always the hard ass. He likes to party, too." He chuckles some more as he opens the door to his building for me, before escorting me up the stairs. We get to the room, and there are so many people!

"So much for just a few people huh, Benny?" I raise my eyebrows at him and he just smirks.

"It's not a party without a ton of people, Short Stack," he says, before pulling me along behind him to where his group of friends are standing by the drinks. I smile and say, 'hi', before grabbing myself a bottle, which I nurse, whilst hoping Ty gets here soon. I don't really know anyone but Benny here and I feel so uncomfortable.

Casting my eyes around the room, I search out faces I might know – there's a very drunk Peter across the room. I've not seen him since the memorial. He was a mess, especially after everything that happened at prom. Our eyes meet and the transformation from sad drunk to angry drunk is instant. I flinch, just seeing the look on his face. He heads towards me, and I see Benny out the corner of my eye assessing the situation. I catch his eye and shake my head. I can handle Peter, but he crosses his arms across his chest and stays where he is watching him like a hawk anyway.

"You filthy bitch! How dare you show your face here after what you did!" Peter spits at me, and I'm shocked into silence. The venom in his voice is like poison, turning the blood in my veins to ice.

"I don't know what you mean, Peter, I haven't done anything."

"Exactly!" he roars so loud the music seems like background music, and more and more people are turning to watch us. "You fucking did nothing. You laid there and let them take her from me! It's your fault she's dead. You killed her!" I feel the tears prick the corner of my eyes, but I refuse to let them come. I let my anger take hold, rather than my sadness.

"I didn't kill her, you jerkoff. I fought for her! And she wasn't yours anymore either." I poke him in the chest as I speak to him in a lowered voice, forcing him to step back. "You threw her away by sticking it in that piece of trash at prom. You threw her away like she meant nothing to you. You threw her away long before those assholes took her away from ME!" I scream at him. I don't notice I'm crying until I feel my tears splash onto my hands. "You never deserved her. You're a worthless sack of shit!"

I see his fist coming towards my face, but it's on me before I register it fully. He hits me square on the jaw and I

143

fall backwards. He's on me, throwing his fists, when I hear Benny roar. Before he gets chance to intervene I wrap my legs around Peter and flip us, before grabbing his hair and slamming his head down on the floor. I draw my arm back and punch his nose until it shatters. Benny lifts me from him, before I do any major damage.

"Someone get that dickstain out of here!" he yells, standing me on my feet.

"You're going to need some ice on that, beautiful. Luckily, he hits like a girl, no offence, so it shouldn't bruise too bad. Let's go get you something for your face."

I nod, looking over to where Peter has been tossed. He's being escorted outside by Ty and another of Benny's friends. I follow Benny to the kitchen area. He lifts me up and places me on the table before pulling some ice from the freezer.

"I'm not a china doll, ya know, Benny," I smile at him.

"Hush now, little one. I happen to like being the hero, so let me do what I do."

"Uh-huh, the gentle giant." I giggle, then hiss as he puts the bag of ice on my jaw. Son of a mothersucker! That stings like salt in a wound. I guess he cut me when he hit me. I'm sat there for a few minutes, when Ty comes back and heads in my direction. He walks straight up to me, positioning himself in front my legs and meeting my eye. He looks at the bag of ice. His rage is barely contained under his skin.

"It's nothing. Just Benny mothering me. See…" I take the bag of ice off my face and his expression turns thunderous. I place my hand on his chest and feel it heave.

"I'm okay, Ty. See, it's nothing I've not had before." I lean into him, kissing him gently and running my fingers through his hair until I feel him relax into me. I smile at him and he smiles back, kissing me.

"I would've killed him if he hurt you, Addie," Ty says.

"I know – and that's why I love you. You protect me even though I can protect myself."

"I love you, too, baby girl. Want to dance?" he asks.

I follow him to the dance area. The music slows and he circles his arms around me. I lean my head over his heart and get lost in the steady beat of it. We stay this way even when the music gets faster; we are dancing to our own beat. I feel so safe wrapped up in him, like nothing else can go wrong. The music fades away and I pull back and look up into his eyes. The song stops and he smiles at me before pulling me back towards Benny and the guys, who are playing stupid drinking games – all in the name of celebration but I can't help it's also in an attempt to forget the sadness that's gripped us all lately.

In the end, I don't hate the night as much as I expected to, but that could be the effects of the drink, which are beginning to make me feel woozy.

DESCENT

I get Ty's attention and tell him that I'm going back to my room and relief washes over his face.

"Thank God, I can't wait to get you alone. I've been waiting all night," he says grabbing my hand. We say our goodbyes to the group and head outside, but the effect of the fresh air sends my world spinning.

"I think something's wrong with me, Ty. I feel really weird," I say just before I stumble to the ground. He picks me up, and I can't feel my legs. I start to worry; I have no idea what's going on. I've only had a few drinks and I've never reacted like this before.

"I'm sorry, Addie," Ty whispers to me as he begins walking us towards the forest, rather than the dorm.

"What's going on, Ty? Where are we going? I need to go back to my room, or to the med centre."

"I'm so sorry, Addie, but they said if they could have you, they'd leave everyone else alone. It's you they wanted – you're the reason Logan and Livvy were killed."

"Who the hell are they, Ty? Where are we going?" I'm screaming in panic as we head into the forest. Ty's legs are so long that we're crossing the ground so much quicker than I'm used to, and I'm being dragged behind. He doesn't answer me, and I can't fight him. My body betrays me in its uselessness. I'm left fully alert knowing that whatever is coming isn't going to be good. I can't quite believe the betrayal. Part of me still thinks this is all some kind of really bad joke.

"Ty, please, please don't do this." I start crying. The person I fell in love with is betraying me.

When we get to a clearing, he lays me down in the centre of it, then paces back and forth waiting. All I can do is lie there as the drugs deaden my system. He spiked my drink! I can't believe he would hurt me like this.

I have no idea how much time passes before I see Kaden and his Shades; they are the same ones who took Livvy and Logan from me.

"You coward, Tyler. How could you fucking do this! You should be ashamed of yourself. Logan and Livvy would be so ashamed of you right now, you prick!" I cry out.

He turns to me with anger all over his face. I don't recognise him. This isn't the Ty who has cradled me night after night – something's wrong. This doesn't make any sense.

"They'd both still be here if it wasn't for you, you little bitch, so shut your mouth and deal with it!" he shouts. We're so deep in the forest, no one is going to hear me screaming.

"Ty?"

He looks down on me, sneering and that's when the hideous truth hits me – he doesn't love me, he didn't love me – it's all been some terrible illusion.

"Well, isn't this delightful," Kaden says. The sound of laughter gilds his words. "You did well, Tyler, making her

147

fall in love with you. Who would have thought she would be quite so stupid?"

Kaden turns to me and shakes his head, tutting, "Oh, dear, Addie – first rule of survival, don't let emotions blind you."

His attention turns back to Tyler. "You will be rewarded for your loyalty and your success."

Tyler shakes his hand. The deal is struck. "Thank you, Kaden. I hope I have proven myself to you."

"Yes, yes," Kaden says dismissively. "Well, there's still a lot for you to prove."

Tyler nods. "Yes, sure – I'm going to head back to the dorm right now, infiltrate the Red Guard as you planned." He bows then walks away leaving me.

"Ty?" I call after him, sure that somewhere in his heart, he is still my Ty and he won't let this happen.

"Ahhhh, Miss Tate. We meet again. Now unfortunately for you, this meeting won't end as well as the last one did, my dear. This time, we're going to take a little trip," he sniggers. I feel pins and needles shoot through my arms as the feeling comes back into them. I push myself up into a sitting position so I can at least look at him without laying at his feet.

"I don't know what you want with me, but I will never go with you," I spit at him. The wind picks up and I hear the clock tower chime, marking midnight. I'm not as far away as I feared. Maybe Xander will hear me.

He laughs and I can hear the Shades sniggering as they circle me. Kaden flashes towards me and suddenly he's in my face. I feel a sharp prick in my neck.

"Now then, Princess, that should make you sleep for just long enough to take you back," he says. The drug doesn't take effect immediately, although I know I have but moments. I use them as best I can – screaming loudly in the hope Xander or one of the other Vampyrs can hear me. Darkness creeps in, and my head gets stuffy as everything blurs. I hear my name being yelled, but my vision turns hazy as I fall back to the ground. Everything goes dark and I hear the sound of metal on metal, and an unnatural roar fills the air.

I have no idea how much time passes as I fade in and out of consciousness, all I know is that I've been picked up and we're moving. I try to cry out but I have no control over myself as I pass out again.

DESCENT

Chapter Nine

ADDIE

I come around and I'm stiff all over. My head is pounding and the swirling in my stomach makes it hard to keep whatever's in there, down. I start by moving my fingers and toes. The concentration it takes is excruciating and I keep my eyes closed while I do it.

I have no idea where I am, and for right now I want to make sure I'm not broken, before I start dealing with whatever fresh hell I'm in right now. Once I know I can move my arms and legs, I turn my head and slowly open my eyes. I'm surrounded by darkness, which I'm instantly thankful for. I open my eyes further trying to take in my surroundings. I can't see much through the blanket of darkness, but I can see enough to know that wherever the hell I am, is not somewhere I recognise.

I'm lying on a bed, still in my prom dress. Jeez, prom feels like forever ago already. I stretch my arms out and I can't reach either side; the sheets are almost silky soft. Not exactly what I was expecting. I slowly push myself up to a sitting position, hissing at the pain, which courses through my body with the movement. I'm going to fucking kill Ty when I see him next, but I can't focus on that right now, all I can do is hope I'm somewhere safe. I'm not going to hold my breath for that.

I lean over to the bedside table and turn on the lamp. It illuminates the room with a soft glow and I gasp at my surroundings. The walls are bare stone brick, with cast iron candle holders attached at various places across the walls, each holding a blood red candle. The room is pretty bare, other than the bed and the table. There are three doors to the right-hand side of the bed, and floor to ceiling black velvet curtains cover the entire wall to my left.

I swing my legs over the side of the bed and discover that I must be about four feet up in the air. Scooting further off the bed, I try and make the fall a little softer, and fail miserably. There's a loud thud as I land and pain shoots up my legs making me want to cry out. I bite my lip to stop the scream and taste blood as it splits.

I grasp onto the bed and try to pull myself up, my limbs shaking from the exertion. Once stable, I pad over the thick carpet to the door closest to me. There's a bathroom on the other side of it, containing an oversized mirror. I don't want to see my reflection but it's hard to miss. The lack of light makes me look ghostly so I turn and focus back on the room. I need to get out of here and I'm searching for any possible escape route. There's nothing here but a luxurious bath suite. No windows.

The next door I try is locked and I'm too weak right now to try and fight it. Admitting defeat, I head to the last door and find a massive walk in closet. I don't spend long investigating, just long enough to know it's full of someone's clothes and that this is someone's room. I just wish I knew who that someone was. I feel my strength waning, what little I had when I woke up has deserted me and I feel exhausted. I fight through it, walking across the room to the wall of black velvet and look for a separation in the fabric. I find it and tug it as much as I can, revealing floor to ceiling windows overlooking a vast lake surrounded by thick forest. It looks like something from a different world.

It must be the middle of the night because the sky is inky black, illuminated by a full glowing moon reflecting across the huge lake. It's beautiful. I sink to the floor staring out of the window. I'm no longer at the Academy and it's all I can do not to cry, because this can only mean that wherever I am, it is where Kaden wants me to be. An overwhelming sense of dread settles deep in my bones, making my already weary body deplete of all energy. I rest my head against the velvet curtain and close my eyes, hoping it's all a bad dream.

DESCENT

The door opens and there is the rustle of material as someone walks into the room. I keep my eyes closed and remain deathly still. I figure if they think I'm asleep or passed out over here, they won't kill me, right? No fun if there's no reaction, and I'm too weak to fight them right now.

"Pretending to be asleep isn't going to help you, you know? I'll drag you into the shower either way," a husky voice laden with venom and hate speaks to me.

I open my eyes to see a woman with long red hair and piercing green eyes. *Vampyr* I think to myself, except she doesn't look like a shade, she looks more like Kaden. I'm beginning to think they skipped something in our History of the Races class because something just isn't adding up. I lift my chin defiantly and meet her eyes. Hatred pours from her like a tsunami and washes over me. I have no idea why this bitch hates me so much, but I sure as shit am not going to let her know it bothers me.

"Yeah, I'd like to see you try," I reply. Way to go, Addie, taunt the Vampyr. Super idea. I face palm internally. Not letting her bother me is one thing, but antagonising her is a whole new realm of bad idea.

She barks out a laugh and crosses her arms. "He said you were feisty. I like feisty, it's more fun when you break. Now get in the damn shower, you smell like vomit," she says pulling a face before turning on her very pointy heel and leaving the room, slamming the door behind her.

154

I flinch at the loud bang and the creaking of the wood. I don't hear the click of a lock, so I assume she's my new guard dog, stood outside waiting for me. *I don't stink. Do I?* I lift the fabric of my dress to my face and gag. *What the hell!* I strip faster than a ghost can say boo and dart towards the bathroom.

I flick the switch and my eyes bounce from the giant tub, to the shower. Although the bath is tempting, sitting in my own stench is not. I head to the shower, the steam rising almost immediately. Despite my anxiety about being held captive, there is no denying the luxurious effect of the power jets on my skin. Reluctantly, I step out of the shower and wrap myself in towels, catching a glimpse of myself in the mirror. I think I might be in shock. My face looks deathly pale even by my standards. I should be freaking out right around now. I mean hell, Tyler has completely sold me out, and I'm now being held by the guy who killed my best friend in front of me, but I'm numb. I literally can't feel a thing. There's no anger, no sadness, no betrayal, and I don't like it. I like that I can function and think clearly, but I know I should be afraid; and I'm not.

I walk back into the bedroom and sit on the bed and before I can fully dress, the door opens again and Kaden strides into the room like he owns the place, *which I guess, he kind of does,* with a smile adorning his face. He looks me over, taking his time, like he's the predator and I'm his prey. *He freaking wishes!* His blonde hair brushes his shoulders, and his blue eyes pierce me as if they see right through me. He's tall, somewhere over six foot, and he is built like a house. His black t-shirt hugs his chest and arms and tapers off at his waist, but I can still clearly see his defined torso under it. His worn blue jeans enhance his strong legs. *Why do the jerks always have to be so pretty?*

"Adelaide, how lovely of you to join us, in your finery no less," he chuckles. *Dick.*

"It's not like I had much choice in the matter, asshole. What the hell am I doing here?"

"Oh, Addie! Patience is a virtue. All will become clear in time. Now my dear, please make yourself at home. I'm sure you'll find something comfortable to wear in the closets. Celeste, the redhead you met earlier, had a wonderful time making sure the room would be ready for you." He grins again and I just want to wipe the smug smile off his face. As much as I am annoyed by him, I'm grateful that he has at least elicited some kind of feeling.

"Oh, remind me to thank her," I say, sarcasm dripping from my words. "And while I'm at it, I'll ask her for a mani-pedi; we can have some real girl time; maybe she'll be my new bestie, ya know, since you killed my other one!"

I swear I see him flinch a little, but it's probably a figment of my imagination. This guy doesn't give a shit about anything.

"That wasn't me, Addie. You had a chance to save her, remember that. Just try to remember that not everything is what it seems," he sighs, and I almost feel bad for him, except apparently my anger is back, because my skin feels on fire. Had a chance to save her my ass!

"A chance to save her?! You're kidding right?" I spit out at him jumping to my feet. He sighs and walks towards me. He lifts his hand towards my face, and tucks a stray strand of hair behind my ear almost tenderly. His movement shocks me and I slap away his hand. "Don't you dare touch me!"

"I'm not the bad guy here, Addie, maybe one day you'll see that." He sighs and turns away, walking towards the door.

"Kaden, you are the bad guy. You are the definition of the bad guy, and if you can't see that then you're deluded."

His eyes flash at my words, a mixture of anger and sadness.

"Believe what you want to, Addie. You'll understand one day. Now please, get dressed and come downstairs for dinner. Celeste will escort you, and don't keep me waiting."

He closes the door behind him and all I can hear is my shallow, heavy breaths from the anger built up inside. I close my eyes and lie back, trying to control my breathing to long deep breaths, trying to dampen the anger swirling inside me. He wants me to go down for dinner? It's the middle of the freaking night! Is he insane? I don't want to eat, but head over to the closet and rummage through the drawers until I find a pyjama set of shorts and vest. He was right; they're exactly my size, and they still have the tags on. I don't want to accept a thing from him, but right now it's that or naked. I rip the tags off and slip into the set before making my way to the vanity section, where there is a variety of hair brushes, hair dryer and straighteners. Anyone would think I was a guest not a freaking prisoner. I sigh, sitting down and working through the knots from my freshly washed hair before drying it. I almost look myself again. Almost. Something's not quite right, but I can't put my finger on it.

Weariness overcomes me and I almost fall to the floor as I stand. I lean onto the wall to keep me upright, waiting for my legs to stop shaking. *This is exactly why I'm not going down for dinner at stupid o'clock.* I slowly work my way back to the bed and slip between the sheets, looking out over the lake as sleep takes me.

XANDER

"Where the hell is she?!" I roar. "I have two critically injured Elite, one possibly dying, a student in chains, but no one can tell me what the hell happened to her!" I slam my fists down onto my desk and I hear the wood split. My rage washes over me and I struggle to rein it in. If anything happens to her, I swear Kaden will beg me for death.

"It's just like I told you, Xander," Dimitri explains. "I saw her leave the party with Tyler and something didn't feel right. I followed them, keeping my distance in case it was nothing, but then I saw him pick her up and knew something wasn't right, so I called for Lex and Bray. They got Ali and Gunner, then found me. By the time they reached me, there was almost nothing we could do. Tyler had basically handed Addie over to Kaden. She had been drugged, so she couldn't fight back. He had a few Shades

159

with him by his side but there were another few dozen hidden in the forest. By the time we had fought through the Shades, Kaden was gone, and so was Addie. Gunner hunted down Tyler and took him straight down to the cellar, Ali took Lex and Bray to medical, and I came here to you."

I can see his anger threatening to burst through, it is rare for my kind to lose their control but we are both close to the edge, and that is dangerous, for us, and for Kaden.

"We need to do some recon, Dimitri. Send out the strike team, everyone needs to go out and speak to their people. We need to find her, as quickly and quietly as possible. No one can know about this; you understand? *No one!"*

"I get it, Xander, but what is so important about her? Don't get me wrong, you know how I feel about her, but what makes her so important that you're willing to risk the lives of everybody else?" he asks.

I have no idea how to tell him, without telling him. She has to know first. She has to know about everything.

"D, I can't tell you much, but you need to know she's different. Special. One of a kind special, and Kaden cannot have her. You know where she'll end up, who she'll end up with if he has her for long. She's too important for that to happen, so much could go wrong. She needs to know the truth, the real truth," I say.

His eyes go wide. It was agreed after the Dark War that some things would be kept from the humans, for their own good. Each leader made a blood oath on behalf of their houses, the Vampyrs for their syrelines, and I for those of my kind who are led by me.

"What the hell! We can't tell her. She is human, that breaks every decree we ever agreed to."

"She's not human, Dimitri. That's as much as I can tell you. We need to get her back. We need to get her back before too much damage is done. Damage that even I can't undo."

I can see him reeling from my admission, but I don't have time to worry. If I'm right, we don't have much time to get her back before it's too late. The cloaking spell will start lifting, and without the right guidance, I don't even want to think about what could happen. They could poison her against us, and with the lies she's been told, I wouldn't blame her for believing them. I know Dimitri has understood the gravity of the situation from the stance he's taken. He is the warrior from The Dark War. My second in command. My brother.

"Please, brother. Help me."

"Of course," he says, before nodding and leaving the room.

I punch the wall and the stone shatters around me. I compose myself before making my way down to the basement. Tyler, the little shit, has pissed me off for the last time. I've always known I didn't like him, but now, betraying her the way he has? He is going to regret it for as long as I see fit to let him live. As I work my way down the spiral, stone staircase, I try to calm my temper. The boy cared for her, I'm sure of it, so there has to be a pretty big reason for his betrayal, *not that I can think of anything worthy enough to betray someone you love.* I reach the bottom of the staircase and look down the long corridor. It was created to intimidate, that much is obvious, the damp grey space is dimly lit by torches. It's cold and bleak, and each footstep echoes, creating eerie sound of four, meaning you can't shake the sense of not being alone. I take a deep breath and try not to imagine the sort of place Addie is in right now. I need a clear head before I go in there. God, Dammit! Why wasn't I here? The guilt washes over me again. *Fuck it!* This son of a bitch isn't going to know what's hit him.

"My patience is wearing thin, Tyler. I'm at the end of being nice. Every second you dick me around is another second of God knows what for Addie. Not that I expect you to care, but if you don't start sharing, real soon, you're going to realise I'm really not a nice guy," I say.

His nose is already broken, and his left eye is swelling. Blood runs down his face onto his shirt, the red seeming so much more startling against the white material. I have no emotion about any of it. I wasn't lying to him – this is me being *nice*. I've been down here for nearly a fucking hour trying to find out where she is, and this dickhead hasn't said a word.

"I don't know what to tell you, man, I don't know where she is. I don't know anything," Tyler moans.

"I don't believe you. I know you're lying to me, Tyler. Why would you want to hurt her like this?"

I see him sneer, and I know I've reached him.

"That little bitch had it coming; leading me on all these years, and then sneaking around with you behind my back. Don't act like it didn't happen – I know. You're a dirty Vampyr and she was all over you. Running with you every day, crying on your shoulder. God only knows what else, it's just wrong! And then my two best friends die – Because OF HER!" he roars. It's like he's been taken over by a wilder version of himself. "That whore deserves to die! I hope they draw it out, make her suffer just like they did. I hope she remembers that I helped them. I'll never tell you anything. She's where she belongs!" he spits.

"You have no idea what you're on about. Unfortunately for you, I know her, I know them, and this isn't going to end well for you. Don't say I didn't warn you."

DESCENT

I press my hands to the sides of his head, and start wading through the dark and murky mess that are his memories. It's harder because he's hurt – but fuck it! I close my eyes and focus on the images in front of me, slowing them down. I can see them after the first attack, the edges of the memory already framed in shades of grey. Guilt. I go further back and that's when I see it.

Tyler and Kaden. Together. In the town, shit, that must have been the day they all went shopping for prom. I can hear them talking and I let the memory play out in my mind.

"I know this is unusual for you, Tyler, but believe me when I say we've been watching you for some time. I'm not associated with the Academy or the Red Guard. My organisation is… Let's say an alternative option to the one you've been made to think is the only one. Most of what you've been taught is the truth, but I know, like me, you've noticed the holes in the histories you've been taught. Things that just don't add up. That's because they don't. You've been lied to almost your entire life Tyler, and my Commander wants you to know the truth. Are you ready for the truth Tyler?"

"I don't know, man. This is all a little weird, some guy I don't know accosts me while I'm away from The Academy for the first time in, well, forever, and wants me to believe in some massive conspiracy; that my parents,

my teachers, my peers have all lied to me. You'll have to excuse my scepticism." He stands and turns to leave when Kaden grabs his arm.

"What if I could prove it? What if I could show you the truth?" Kaden asks.

"And how the hell would you do that?" Tyler asks.

"Sit back down and I'll show you," Kaden says, letting go of his arm.

Tyler sits back down and Kaden touches his wrist then closes his eyes. Tyler's eyes go wide and his nose starts bleeding. Shit!

"What the hell was that? How did you do that?" Tyler asks, wiping the blood from his nose.

"That, Tyler, was just a hint of the truth," Kaden says with a triumphant dirty smirk on his face, knowing he's won this battle.

"I can't believe… how did you do that? That just… Why would they lie about that?"

"Because they can, because keeping humans in the dark is what they've always done. I can show you more of the truth, Tyler. I can teach you so much, but I need to know you're with us."

Tyler looks uncertain for a minute before resolve paints his features. The anger at being kept in the dark, the thirst for the truth and the power that comes with it. "I'm in."

DESCENT

"Good. Now I'm convinced, but he will need you to prove it to us...."

I finish the rest and exit the memories, releasing Tyler's head. FUCK! I knew they'd play dirty, but this? And this little insect thinking he could endanger her, without even questioning it. What a fucking screw up! He really doesn't know a thing about why they wanted her! I look over at him, passed out from me sifting through his mind. Since he knows the truth, I won't bother to wipe him. There's no point.

Kaden had to know we'd take him after she was taken. Could he really know who she is? A long time ago, Kaden and I were friends, and I'd like to think he'd never be able to pass her over to his Commander if he knew who she really is. Would he? I hate not knowing any of this.

I leave the basement and head back up to my office. I can only hope Dimitri has had more success than I have.

Chapter Eleven

ADDIE

I have no idea what time it is when I feel the covers being ripped off of me.

"What the freaking hell!" I squeak darting to cover myself, the t-shirt I'm in isn't doing a great job of covering me.

"Wakey, wakey, sweetheart," Celeste purrs standing at the end of the bed, her eyes raking over my body. Uncomfortable much! My discomfort must have shown because a dirty smirk crosses her face. "Oh sweetheart, you'd better get used to this. Being that delicious and innocent in this crowd will get you devoured." She laughs and walks over to the window.

I've been in here on my own for what feels like weeks now, with food and drink being brought to me occasionally. If it wasn't for the window, I wouldn't know how long I've been here. This might be a fancy cage, but it is still a cage, and I need to remember that. No matter how nice these people appear, they kidnapped me and I still had no idea why.

"What the hell do you want?" I ask, faking more confidence than I feel. I get up and look her in the eyes. My arms crossed over my chest.

She grins wickedly. "Well now, sugar; we've got to get you ready for your debut party."

"I'm not going to any stupid party. I want to go home. Why am I even here?"

"Tut, tut, sweetheart. You're asking all the wrong questions. You'll see in time. Now go clean up so we can make you the treat of the ball," she says in that honey voice, which makes shivers run down my spine. I don't know who she is, but I know she's dangerous.

"I already told you, I'm not going to your stupid party, so you might as well just leave me the hell alone," I spit out. Faster than I can blink, she's on me, her hand around my neck lifting me off the floor. I claw at her hand and kick out at her, but it's like she's made of steel, she can't feel a thing.

"Now listen here, you ungrateful brat, your life could be much fucking worse right now. Kaden is being a very gracious host. Too fucking gracious if you ask me, and you dare throw it in his face? Now you're going to do exactly as I say and get ready, and then you're going to put on a smile – fake it if you have to, and make everyone believe you're having the night of your fucking life. Do you get me?" she whispers, her face inches from mine. I try to nod but can barely move. She drops me to the floor.

My feet are too unsteady to catch me and I crumble to a pile on the floor. I gasp for air and it almost hurts when it fills my lungs. I look up and she's back by the window. *Fucking Vampyrs and their speed. Assholes!* How fucking dare she treat me like this! I shouldn't be here. I haven't a clue as to what I'm doing here, and after leaving me for days, I almost hoped no one would come back.

I prayed for a search party, but nothing. Maybe Tyler got away. Maybe they think I ran off with him. What if no-one is coming? Panic grips me and I feel the bile rise in my already battered throat. I run to the bathroom to puke up what little is left in my stomach. As I hug the ceramic bowl, hopelessness tries to creep in on my senses. *Not a fucking chance.* There is no way I'm giving up. I've spent the last four days trying to think of a way to escape, but even if I could get out of here, I'd have to cross the lake to get to civilisation, but it's a big lake, and its seriously cold out there. I don't know if I'd survive. I flush the chain and splash my face with cold water. I look into the mirror. Man, was that a bad idea? Red rings are forming around my neck, matching my red bloodshot eyes.

Celeste marches into the room, her heels clicking on the tiled floor. She stares at me with a scowl.

DESCENT

"You might be pretty sweetheart, but you really need to work on that charm of yours if you want to survive around here. Being a bitch will only get you so far," she says before walking back into the main room.

I take a deep breath and psyche myself up to deal with the monster in my room. *Why can't they stay hidden under the bed?* I can get through this; I know I can. These past few months have been horrendous, but I survived. If I can survive losing Livvy, I can handle these assholes. I take another deep breath and walk through the door into what looks like an explosion of clothing. There are rails and rails of dresses, along with rows upon rows of shoes.

What the hell! Okay, maybe I can't handle this. I have no idea what the hell is going on anymore.

"Erm… Celeste?"

"Yes?"

"What is all of this?"

"I told you, we're having a party. This is you getting ready."

I look around at everything and despair tugs at me. Only twice in my life have I dressed up like this. Prom with Livvy, and then… I can't even think about it. Tears threaten to spill. I wipe them away and pull on my metaphorical big girl panties. Maybe the best thing to do is to play along? A party might mean an opportunity to escape.

I walk over to the dressing table and throw myself onto the stool waiting there. A knock on the door startles me. I turn to see a face peeping around the door. The squeal, which comes from its owner shocks me more than anything I think I've ever seen or heard.

"Oh my God Celeste!" he says. "You didn't tell me she was so delicious! The girls and boys are going to weep in delight with this one," he says clapping his hands together. He stands at about six foot, with electric blue hair, shaved on one side from the parting. On the other side of his parting, his hair is long and flicked over the shaved side. It's weird - like a Mohawk gone wrong, but it looks epic. He's in a pair of leather pants and that's it. His skin is covered in ink that almost looks like it's alive. The patterns accentuate the muscles of his torso. He's lean and toned, and just downright beautiful. What is it about these bloody Vampyrs? Why can't any of them be hideous? It's really not fair on the rest of us!

Celeste laughs as he walks towards me. I turn away, trying to hide my blushes, but he can see me in the mirror. I curse how my hormones have betrayed me. I feel him standing behind me and he winks through the mirror.

"Hey there, gorgeous, I'm Michael, and believe me, the pleasure is all mine! Just look at this beautiful clean slate I get to play with!" he squeaks, running his fingers through my hair. I flinch.

171

DESCENT

"You can't play with it too much. Kaden gave me orders," Celeste says. His whole body droops with disappointment.

"What a party pooper," he sighs. "Well, I guess I'll just find other ways to play," he says grabbing the straighteners. I sit as he moulds my hair to his will and then spins me around to apply makeup to my face. I have no idea how long he's been preening, but when he stands back and claps his hands together, I know he's done. Celeste leers at me approvingly. I go to turn and look in the mirror when Celeste yells, "Wait!"

I stop as she jumps to her feet and heads over to one of the rails, pulling off a long black dress - although I call it a dress sparingly, there's hardly anything to it.

"Oh, hell no," I protest, shaking my head and putting up my hands. "I cannot wear whatever the hell that is."

Celeste smirks that dirty smirk again, and I know my fight is already lost. She's already proven once today that she can overpower me, I could do without any more bruises. Besides, I get the feeling I'm going to need all my strength later for whatever the hell this party is.

"Fine, give it to me," I sigh and she hands me the dress. I can hear Michael's excitement behind me, oozing out of his pores. I've never known such an excitable Vampyr. I look at him then to the dress, wondering if I should just head to the bathroom to get changed.

"Oh, doll, don't you worry your pretty little head; you've got the wrong bits to make me hot. It's not me you need to worry about," he chuckles, tipping his head in Celeste's direction, resulting in her throwing one of my pillows at him.

"Shut up, jerk! Addie, just put the goddamn dress on. We don't have all night, you know," she says, before stalking back into the closet. I step into the dress. I guess I've been given no bra for a reason. I slide the dress straps over my shoulders and run my hands down the material, earning a wolf whistle from Michael. I turn around and smile at him, he's been nothing but nice to me, even if he does work for that asshole Kaden.

"Oh, sugar, you need to smile more; it lights up your whole being."

I walk over to the mirror and look at my reflection. I hardly look like myself. My hair is in big barrel curls waving down my back, with streams pulled back in twists and red ribbon running through it. My face is pale, with dark smoky eyes and there are silver gems in each corner. The look is finished with blood red lipstick. *I look like one of them,* I think. My dress is a cut out bandage dress, a triangle from the shoulders dipping very far down into my cleavage, with two triangles cut out at my waist, showing off my toned abs. The skirt hugs my thighs, stopping just below the line of my ass. Michael appears behind me, making me seem even shorter than normal, his arm drapes over my shoulder with some blood-red satin peep-toe stilettos.

"These will finish you off perfectly, sugar. Pop them on and we can get this party started." He squeezes my shoulder as I take the shoes from him.

Holy crap these are like stilts!

"Stunning," he whispers in my ear, before stepping away. I think I might like him; he's the nicest person I've come across here yet. And I need someone I can trust; maybe it's him? Maybe he'll help me? Who am I kidding?

Celeste appears from the closet looking like she's ready for a runway.

"I knew hoarding all of those clothes across the centuries would be a good idea!" she says in that sultry, husky tone she seems to take on when she's in a good mood. She's in a full length white dress, which looks like something from the history books I've seen; the Greeks I think. A white rope circles her neck and the material falls like a waterfall down her front to a cinched waist. The effect makes it look like she's floating. Her heeled sandals have white ribbons that run up her calves. Much as I hate to admit it, she looks stunning. The white contrasts with the red of her hair, making her look like a fiery goddess.

"Come on, sweetheart, let's get this show on the road," she says, looking over me approvingly. She strides out of the room and Michael takes my hand and puts it through his arm.

"Come on, doll, best not keep the witch waiting; she's a beast when she's late," Michael whispers with a sparkle in his eye. I flinch a little when I hear Celeste yell at us.

"I can still hear you, asshole!"

Michael laughs and walks me through a maze of corridors, which I can't even begin to try and remember. Escaping is going to be impossible. My shoulders drop.

"None of that, sugar. They'll eat you alive. Chin up for now, and no matter what, keep that game face of yours on tonight," Michael says but it doesn't reassure me at all.

What the hell am I walking into?

We follow Celeste until we arrive at two huge oak doors. She stops and turns to me.

"Good luck in there, sweetheart, you're going to need it. Try not to lose your soul, okay?" she says with such nonchalance I think she's joking, but that's not what she does.

Michael and Celeste walk through the doors, leaving me in the doorway wondering if it's too late to run back to my cage and hide. Surely it's safer in there if the people who kidnapped me are wishing me luck in here?

I take a deep breath and put on the game face Michael spoke of, steeling myself to the horrors through those doors. I take a step into the room and silence descends around me. All eyes are on me. I freeze like a deer in a spotlight before I remember Michael's words. *Game face.* I lift my chin and straighten my shoulders

175

before walking further into the room. I take in everything around me and pretend it doesn't disturb me in every manner as I walk straight to an empty table across the room. I take a seat and pretend I belong. I flick my eyes across the room, not wanting to look at any one thing for too long. There are so many beings in here; I wouldn't even know where to begin. It's then I realise I'm surrounded by Demons. Holy fuck! I try to keep my breaths even as I search the room for someone, anyone I recognise.

Then I see her, a girl who looks about my age staring out at us all like this is the worst night of her life. She's locked in a birdcage, wearing basically nothing, and she looks as terrified as I feel. I get up slowly and make my way towards her, trying not to draw any attention to myself. I'm halfway to her when I hear Kaden.

"There you are, Addie; I was wondering when you'd find me,' Kaden purrs. I turn around to see him in a silver, grey tux and black tie. He looks like a character from a book; perfect and chiselled, except for the cold, which fills his eyes. The warmth he greeted me with days before gone. "Come on, I have some guests to introduce you to," he says, grabbing my waist. His fingers push into my skin just hard enough that I can't fight him. He drags me over to his table and sits me on his lap.

"What the hell do you think you're doing?" I hiss, trying to get out of his grip, but its futile.

"So this is your latest spoils huh, Kaden?" A dark skinned man with silver hair and blue eyes asks.

"Something like that, Lucan. This one is for *him*."

"So why is she here? Surely he'd want to keep all that purity for himself?" he asks, with hunger in his eyes as he looks over me.

Kaden shrugs. "Maybe he wants her a little dirtied up before he gets to her – so she isn't so stiff," he replies before taking a swig of his drink.

"I am here you know. I'm not a mute freaking doll," I say.

"Ooh, she has fire. She's going to be fun to play with," Lucan laughs.

"*She* has a name! And *she* is not a toy. I mean, *I* am not a toy. Jeez! You know what I mean! Regardless, none of you will be dirtying me up, and just as soon as I can, I am outta here," I say, trying to stand but I'm restricted by Kaden's arm wrapped around my stomach. I turn and glare at him, and he looks at me with mischievous eyes. What the hell is his end game? And who the hell is he on about handing me over to? I seriously need to up my escape game.

"Drink, Addie?" Kaden asks with a glint still in his eyes.

"Would it matter if I said no?" I ask him, meeting his eyes with my own. I will not cower in front of him. Not here. He laughs at me and signals to a girl across the

177

room who brings us two glasses. One contains a thick red liquid and it is handed over to Kaden. *Man, I hope that's wine.* And the other, full of a dark brown liquid, is handed to me. Kaden looks at me expectantly and I decide to choose my battles, lifting the liquid to my lips and taking a sip. The sweetness and the bubbles overwhelm me. I've never tasted anything so sweet, and I'm sure the sour look on my face is what causes the entire table to laugh.

"What?" I ask.

"I think, my dear, we all forget how limited your life's experiences have been. It's almost refreshing to see someone new to the real world. There is so much I have to teach you; so much for you to experience," Kaden says, chuckling softly.

I just can't get a read on him. One minute he's hard and unrelenting, and then in others he's soft and sweet. Don't get me wrong, there is always an underlying coldness to him, a darkness visible through his eyes, but just sometimes, that cracks and he makes me wonder why he picked the side he did.

He ignores me and talks to the people at the table, whilst I take in more of the room. There are more of the birdcages I spotted earlier dotted around the room, each holding a girl around my age. They are dressed, if you can even call it that, in skimpy leather underwear in different styles. Some of the cages hang from the ceiling. Those girls look more comfortable in their cages, dancing to the beat of the music, which plays in the background. They want eyes on them.

The people surrounding me are not people I'm used to being around, but I know they're not human. I've studied enough Demon lore to know this room is not full of nice people.

There's a woman with grey skin, long black hair, put up in a high pony tail, with most of her body on display except for a metal type corset, and a chain link skirt. Her ears are pointy, and her eyes make her appear Asian. She's beautiful, in a dangerous type of way. Sexy is probably more apt. Her eyes are a striking green and they appear to glow. The ink covering her body looks like it moves. I realise she's probably a dark Elf; one of the few legions of Fae who sided with the Demon King during the Dark War. I look away, the last thing I want is to draw more attention to myself than necessary but I continue to scan the room. There are Banshees and Gorgons, mixed with human looking Demons, which I can't place. Shades are dotted around the perimeter, their greying skin, and yellowing eyes and nails making them stick out. I look back at the girls in the raised cages and realise they're Succubae; their red glowing eyes give them away.

I feel so freaking overwhelmed right now, I can barely keep my thoughts in order. There are so many different races around me; it's taking everything I can not to freak out. I'm used to Fae and Vampyrs, but the thought of being trapped in a room with this many Demons, and no Red Guard scares the absolute shit out of me. Kaden must notice I've tensed because he leans closer to me and whispers in my ear,

"They won't hurt you, sweetheart. They're not the bad guys."

"Are you freaking kidding me? Not the bad guys? I'm in a room of freaking Demons and *you* kidnapped me!" I hiss.

"Okay, so I'll admit, we've all done not so stellar things, but we're not bad people."

"That's because you're not people!"

"Touché. Regardless, as long as you do what you're told, you won't be harmed. Do you understand me?"

I nod because there's not much more I can do. Kaden returns to his conversation and loosens his hold around my waist. I want to go and find the girl I saw, something about her looked familiar and I want to know why. I tap Kaden's arm and tell him I need to pee and he nods, pointing me in the direction of the toilets. I make out I'm following his directions before detouring to where I saw her earlier. I find her cage and see her sat in the middle, trying to cover herself with her arms. When I walk up to the cage, she starts to cry, backing away from me. She shakes her head at me and waves her arms as if to stop me.

"Please, no, not me. There are so many other girls here who would be better. Just, please, please, don't pick me!" she mutters through her tears. I kneel down to her level and look her in the eyes. Purple. *Holy shit, she's Fae!*

"I'm not going to hurt you, I swear! My name's Addie," I say.

There's a hand on my shoulder and my stomach flips with fear. I look up to see Michael standing above me with a disapproving look. It looks wrong on his face.

"Addie, you shouldn't be here, doll. If Kaden saw you, well, let's not go there. Let's get you back to your table," he says with a sad smile, lifting me to my feet effortlessly.

"Who is she, Michael? And why the hell is she here? Why is she in that cage and absolutely terrified?" I ask.

I can't contain it. I'm furious at them all. How dare they treat her, treat anyone, like this! They might have me held captive, but I'm not out on parade like she is.

"You'll see soon enough, doll. Now you go and sit down," he says, pushing me back towards Kaden.

Kaden sees me and I can see the questions on his face about my new mood. He looks behind me to Michael. I miss his reaction, but from the look now on Kaden's face, I'm going to say it wasn't in my favour! Kaden gets up and raises his hand to me, beckoning me to him. I take a deep breath and walk towards him. He grabs my wrist and sits back down, pulling me down with him. Thankfully, not on his lap this time.

181

DESCENT

"You shouldn't go exploring here, girl. You have no idea where you are."

"Maybe not. But I'm already here against my will, with no idea what the hell I'm doing here, and obviously my every move is being tracked. It's not like I can go far," I say crossing my arms.

Okay, so maybe I look like a brat right now, but I want some answers. "Why am I here, Kaden? Why do you have a Fae locked in a cage? What *is* this place?"

"You're an inquisitive little thing aren't you, girl? I suggest you learn your place and do as you're told. Things could be much worse for you if you'd like?" he says. The look on his face is so cold that he could probably kill me where I sit and have no feeling about it.

Just then, the lights dim and are replaced with light from the table lamps. The music volume increases, and space clears on the floor in front of me. I look around, knowing something dramatic is about to happen. My attention is pulled to the grounded cages and each girl looks terrified. Kaden stands and leaves me at the table; Celeste takes his seat. Her time to baby-sit, I guess. Kaden gets up and stands in the middle of the floor.

"Welcome to the Night Rooms. For those of you who have been here before, you know how the game works. For those of you who have not, stick to the rules – or the game could end… *brutally*," he says with a wicked gleam in his eye. The way the dim light illuminates him makes him appear more than he is. Bigger, scarier, more threatening even. "Enjoy your spoils, and remember – all is fair in love and war."

The lights go out and we're drowned in darkness. Then the music starts so loudly that even though I cover my ears, it still penetrates. Red strobe lights flash. The effect is terrifying. I look around, and all I can see are glimpses of people walking away from my table. I huddle myself into the chair, trying to make myself small. Something really bad is about to happen, I know it. That's when I hear the screams over the music.

I feel a hand on my shoulder and I scream. This place is turning me into a total wuss. I look up and see a face I don't know smiling down at me, and shivers run down my spine.

The smile is not a friendly smile. I try to stand and remove the strangers grip but he holds tighter, keeping me where I am. I grab his wrist and try to pull his hand away from my shoulder. His fingers are digging into my skin so much that it feels like he's going to push through it. I pull harder and the smile leaves his face. He brings his face to mine, so close that I can feel his breath on my lips. Then the bastard licks my face. I'm so grossed out that I forget to be afraid and I punch him square in the jaw - *holy crap my hand!* The impact floors him and I get up and run, the pain in my hand second to my instinct to get away. I see the door and weave through the crowd. I try not to pay attention to what's happening around me, it's like a pool of depravity.

That's when I see the Fae, hidden in the corner of the room trying to stay out of sight. I rush over to her but she pushes herself into the wall, trying to get away. Her purple eyes are pleading with me not to notice her.

"Hey, look, I'm not going to hurt you. My name's Addie, and I'm not here by choice either, but I do have somewhere we can go and get away from all of this. You're just going to have to trust me, okay?" I say hurriedly, looking around making sure no-one has seen me. She nods slowly and I grab her wrist, pulling her behind me. With relief, we're out of the door and in the silence of the corridor.

"Please don't hurt me," she quietly says. Her face is tear stained.

"I swear, I'm not going to hurt you," I say.

Her eyes go wide. *"You can hear me?"*

I look at her with confusion. Her lips didn't move. Holy crap, what sort of Fae is she? I've never heard of one that could project their thoughts.

"Erm, yeah, I guess I did. How did you do that?" I ask, trying not to let the panic take over.

"I didn't do anything. Please, help me."

She reminds me so much of Livvy in this moment that it almost buckles me. Her long blonde hair is dirty and matted and dirt mars her skin. The sight of it pains me deeply. My training starts to kick in. She is my new mission. Keep her safe. I stand up straight and brush myself down.

"I've been trained for the Red Guard, I will do everything I can to protect you," I say and she looks at me sceptically.

"There's never been a girl in The Guard, and if you are in The Guard, how did you end up here?" she asks.

I look around, we can't have much time before people start to notice we're gone.

"I never said I was in The Guard, just that I trained for it. Now are you going to follow me, or do you want to just stand here and wait for them to find us?"

"I'm sorry, you're right. It's just been so long since I've come across someone who isn't trying to use or abuse me, it's hard to trust you, you know. Anyway, I'm Rose, Rose Frostheart. Please tell me you have a way out of here?"

"Nope, sorry, no way out. But I have somewhere safer than here," I say with much more confidence than I feel.

"Hold on, did you say Frostheart? As in the Royal Fae family from the Isles, Frostheart?" she nods.

Holy crap! No pressure Addie.

The maze to get down here was so intricate, I have no idea if I can make it back to where they have been keeping me without someone finding us. I just want to get

185

her back, get her clean, and let her sleep. If someone finds us, then well I'll deal with that when it happens.

"Come on, let's go," I command.

Chapter Twelve

XANDER

I look at the warriors around the table in front of me – my Elite, and I wonder how it is possible that between the eight of us we can't find one girl. We have toppled empires and destroyed legions of Demons, but we can't find Addie. The faces looking back at me share the same frustration but that doesn't change the fact we're failing.

"How is it that no-one knows where Kaden is? Surely he's not so well hidden; someone must be helping him. Does anybody have an update? Even a whisper or a lead?" I ask, trying to keep the desperation from my voice.

"Xander, we have nothing. We've had nothing for weeks; we can't keep putting all of our resources into finding just one girl. We have bigger matters to focus on. We've had two attacks here, one ending up in a captive – if she's even still alive. We need to go about protecting here and the Valoires'," Rome says.

DESCENT

I look into his pitch black eyes and see that he doesn't understand the gravity of the situation. "Rome, you have fought alongside me ever since The Fall. You should know by now that I don't do anything without reason. He wants her for something. We have no idea what, but I can almost guarantee that whatever it is, it's not going to end well for us. You know as well as I do, exactly who Kaden answers to these days. He's not calling the shots, he's following orders. And, I for one, don't want to be the one who just kicks this aside and let's their plan play out.

"Well, we're not going to get any answers just sitting here," Dimitri says, standing from the table and walking over to the cabinet in the corner of the room. He reaches into one of the cupboards and pulls out a bottle of bourbon, then grabs a tower of glasses and brings them over to the table, pouring out a shot for all of us.

"We all need a break," he says, eyeing me with a steely look. "There has been a constant threat of late, and not one of us has had time to catch a breath." He tips the drink back and smiles at us.

This is why he will always be my right hand, he reads people so well, and seems to know exactly what to do to help everyone. The tone of the room changes and everyone relaxes, and it feels like it did before, before the Dark War.

Back then, we were hidden; it was an entirely different world. The humans were thriving. It was the age of technology and the world was paradoxically expanding at the same time it was becoming smaller. It was the time of the Internet and mobile phones; the world was our oyster.

I have been on this earth for thousands of years, and watching it bloom and destroy itself has been a never-ending cycle, but, 'The Outbreak' was different. It was almost like the world was trying to revert itself, to the way it was before The Fall. I shudder when I think of it. The way it rampaged across the world, wiping out millions of people, indiscriminate in its choosing of victims.

The death of so many affected us all. It is one of the reasons I chose for my syreline to stand with the Fae – they wanted to restore the world to its natural glory; to revel in the beauty and wonders the world can provide. Some of them have been here longer than I have. They come from the earth and they worship it, drawing their powers from it. I wanted to bring all that back, and Cole didn't want that – he wanted to rule and destroy what little was left of humanity. His vision of the world was twisted; he wanted to punish those who made him hide in the Old World. If he'd had his way, humans would have been his slaves, so would the Fae. His selfish reasoning's were not enough to sway me, or thankfully, most of my brothers. The five who sided with him, of which Kaden is one, once fought side by side of us – we were brothers in arms, and now he fights for the very thing that goes against our nature. He seeks to destroy rather than build, still bitter about our lives after The Fall and how we had to hide from the humans. His views aligned with Cole's almost completely. I wasn't surprised when I learned of his betrayal, but I was still disappointed.

"Brother, don't look so glum," Dimitri says to me across the table, pulling me from my thoughts. I look at those around me and see the jovial looks on their faces. He's right. I need to dedicate this night to them. Celebrate the wins of late rather than focus on the losses. I lift my glass to them and sip the bourbon, welcoming the burn it brings.

I listen to them laugh and joke about times before The Dark War, the stupid bar brawls they'd have just for the fun of it.

Dimitri laughs at Zero, "Do you remember that one time you wanted to duel for the right to take that red headed whore to bed? Man, you drank way too much that night!"

Aliana jumps in, "Still not as bad as the time Rome nearly took my head off with his new fucking axe. Showing off like he was Thor. I still say you carry that shit to make up for short comings!" She laughs and everyone laughs with her.

"Xander, do you remember that one night, back at the beginning, when that pack of wolves thought they could run us out of their town. I thought that poor kid was going to piss himself when you showed him who you were!" Dimitri says. I can't help but laugh at the memories.

Before The Dark War, things weren't great, but they weren't as serious as they are now. Now we're running around trying to stop the world from killing itself. We're fighting people who we once considered our brothers and sisters. I think back to how Kaden and I were before all of this; thick as thieves, together we were unbeatable. We brought down dictatorships and helped people without them even knowing it.

Of course, we had our differences, but what brothers don't? It pains me to think where he is now. And while I'm as close to my Elite as could be, Kaden was my brother, my *real* brother, and knowing how far he has fallen, the things he is capable of...

I try and shake off my morose feelings and join in the memories being passed around the table. Booze always did make this lot rowdy.

The hours' tick by and I'm only half here, the other half of me is thinking about Addie. We didn't have enough time before. I never got the chance to talk to her properly. Not how I would have liked to. I know she knows I'm here to protect her, but she doesn't understand just quite how protective of her I feel, of how I feel, full stop.

If we manage to find her, I swear I'll make sure she knows. It can't be too hard, right? To tell her that she means more to me. I just need things to stop getting in the way. I need to find a time to tell her the truth about me, about us, and hope she can forgive me. It is forbidden, but I can't keep lying to her, not if I want her to trust me.

A knock pounds on the door and it bursts open.

"My Liege! You need to come to the front gates at once!" A Vampyr from the guard says. "We saw them coming from the distance, from the direction of the tower. At first, we weren't sure but now we are. You need to see. You wouldn't believe me if I told you." The look on his face is all I need to make me get to my feet. My Elite stand with me, ready for battle, the warriors they are coming through in an instant.

"Let's go."

Chapter Thirteen

ADDIE

"Are you sure we're safe in here?" Rose asks. I brought her back to my room after wandering around the corridors of this place, trying to work our way back. Once I calmed her, I encouraged her to shower, promising I would keep guard and let no-one in. I don't know exactly how she's been living, but I can only imagine what she's been through being held here. Afterwards, she looked like a totally different person. I gave her a pair of pyjamas from the closet, figuring she'd want to cover up. I was right, she looked at me like she was going to cry in gratitude for being given clothes, real clothes. I let her dress, then sat her down and brushed her hair and dried it before she curled up on the bed. I thought she might sleep but she just lay there and stare out of the window.

"I've not been hurt in all the weeks I've been here," I say. "I will make sure you receive the same treatment. I won't let them hurt you again," I mean it. I will fight Kaden, Michael or Celeste. I don't care who finds us, she will not go back to the way she was living. No-one deserves to live like that.

"Thank you, Addie. Thank you more than you'll ever know. No one has ever shown me such kindness. You are truly one of the best people I have ever known." She breaks my heart. Everyone should know kindness.

"What about your parents? Your family and friends? Surely someone is looking for you?" She turns to me and the sadness in her features floors me.

"I fear my family gave up on me long ago. I have been gone from them for so long that I doubt they even believe I am still alive."

"You're not from around here, are you?" I ask.

"No, I am from far across the ocean. My family rules over what was once known as England and Europe. My older brother is probably on the throne by now. I miss him terribly."

"You speak like my friend, Xander. Well, I say friend, he's… He's a Vampyr, like Kaden and the rest, but he's nice. He's so kind and sweet, giving and protective," I sigh. *But he's still not found me.*

"Xander? As is Xander Bane?" she asks, the light in her eyes illuminating her entire face.

"Yes, you know him?"

"Not really, he and my brother were friends long ago. I doubt he even remembers me but before I came here, I met him. He stayed with our family for a while – before 'The Outbreak'. He is your friend?"

"Yes."

"So he might be looking for you?" The hope in her eyes shines so brightly that I hate to disappoint her.

"I had hoped so, but I've been here for weeks, and well, I'm still here and he isn't, so…" I sigh. "It's down to me to get us out of here."

At that moment, my door bursts open, banging against the wall so hard I think the door may shatter. Rose falls off of the bed and cowers behind it as Kaden stalks into the room. The rage on his face is obvious.

"ADELAIDE!" he roars. I want to wince but I will not cower to him, not again.

"Yes, Kaden?"

"Don't you play stupid with me, Addie. Where is she?"

"She's safe, and that's exactly where she's staying! How dare you treat her, treat anyone like that! It's disgusting. You should be ashamed of yourself. You try to make yourself appear like a decent person but you can't hide from me, Kaden; I've seen what you're capable of. You're an abhorrent beast, and you sicken me. Your actions are despicable, and that *game* of yours. The depravity, the hunger, I have no words for it!"

195

DESCENT

"You test my patience, girl. She belongs to me! You will give her to me, now!"

"I will do no such thing! She is not your property, she is a person, a Fae no less! She is someone you should be protecting, not submitting to torture, even if it's at another's hands. She will be staying here with me. You can fight me if you must, but you've seen me fight for what I hold dear, and I know that for some reason you don't want me hurt. This is not something I'm going to let up on, Kaden so you might as well accept it."

I can almost see him shake. The anger takes hold of him and his eyes flash red. Fear roots me in place but I won't let him see it. I will not let him take anyone else from me, goddamn it! He already took Logan and Livvy, and Tyler. I have lost too much to him. As I think it, I see remorse flash in his eyes and he looks at me defeated.

"So be it. She is your responsibility, and you will be held accountable for her," he says, before storming out of the room slamming the door behind him.

I slump down onto the bed in relief, the adrenaline leaving almost instantly. Rose climbs up behind me and hugs me.

"Thank you so much, Addie. I am, and will forever be, in your debt."

I wake up a few days later with Rose wrapped around me, which is something I've had to get used to. It's this or the screams in the middle of the night.

The first night, I thought someone had broken into the room and was trying to drag her away. I woke up ready to take anyone on. The next thing I knew, Michael and Celeste were in the room, swords out ready to take on anyone. The amusement on Michael's face equally matched the fury on Celeste's. Since then, she's slept wrapped around me, and Michael has been camped on a make shift bed by the door. It's not been great for me, the little privacy I had, has been destroyed, but it's worth it for her. I wouldn't change it.

Plus, I think Michael loves being on watch with us. He joins in Rose's silly games, and does our hair. He's like our missing third.

I've entirely given up hope of being rescued. I've been here too long. If they're still looking for me, I'll be amazed. I'm sure The Guard have more to worry about than one missing human. I miss Xander and Dimitri, more than I thought I would, and not even for the reasons most would think. I miss running with Xander in the mornings, and fighting with Dimitri in the afternoons. Training isn't

197

something I've been able to do here, even running, and I can feel the detrimental effects on my body already. I try to stretch, and Michael's been doing something called yoga with us, which has helped to keep me lithe, but I want to run and feel the wind. I just want to go outside.

I slide out from Rose's hold, and gently walk past Michael to the bathroom. I close the door and sigh as I lean against it. Alone at last. I turn the shower on and as the room fills with steam I undress, feeling my body relaxing.

I step under the water and let it wash over me. It's here I can be myself and let go. I can think of all the things I can't think about when there's people around. Like the fact it's nearly my birthday, and Livvy won't be here for it. I don't remember ever having had a birthday where she didn't manage to round up cupcakes or cookies to celebrate, even when I didn't want to. The fact she's gone and the people here are the reason makes me angry. Then there is Kaden. I really don't know how to read him. Since I've been here, he's mostly been nice to me, kind almost, aside from the odd occasion where he's been his alter-ego Kaden the monster.

Then there is Logan gone. He would have been so disappointed in Ty. They all would have been. Most of all, I'm disappointed in Ty, but despite his betrayal, there's a part of me that still... No, I shake those thoughts away. I don't even know what happened to Ty after he handed me over. Everything overwhelms me and the sobs wrack my body as I slide to the floor; the water drowning my tears.

Michael bang's on the door but I can't bring myself to answer him. I'm drowning in the facts of everything. I've not let myself think of Livvy much while I've been here, but Rose reminds me of her so much, and thinking of her tears my heart to shreds. I miss Livvy so damn much. I hear a crash as the bathroom door opens, and then Michael is in front of me with a towel. He turns off the water, gathers me up and sits me on his lap, stroking my hair.

"It's going to be okay, sweetie; you'll get through this. I'm here."

It takes everything I have to swallow the anger that rises – at him, at Kaden, at all of them who took her from me.

"I know, honey. I know. I can feel every single ounce of your pain. Every drop of heart break. I'm sorry he took her from you, I am so sorry," he says, rocking me back and forth.

The tears slow and I see Rose opposite us, tears running down her face.

"I'm so sorry, Addie. I didn't know."

I shake my head. "You have nothing to be sorry for, Rose."

I look at Michael and he nods, a small sad smile on his face. He knows I can't say the same for him. I stand, securing the towel around me and move back into the bedroom. Rose follows me, and Michael leaves the room. Seconds after he closes the door, Celeste's head peers around, just to remind us we're not alone - and I swear I almost see guilt on her face. She closes the door, leaving us to our sadness.

I get up and get dressed in jeans and a t-shirt, pulling my hair back in a ponytail, and putting on the converse sneakers and leather jacket I have adopted since being there – thankful again to the Fae for keeping alive some of the clothing from the Old World. Rose follows suit and asks me to braid her hair, which I do absentmindedly staring out of the window. The things I'd do to be out there.

"Are you okay, Addie?" Rose asks, and I nod.

"I am. I lost someone close to me not long ago because of Kaden, and I miss her, every single day."

We continue talking about The Academy and everything that's happened to me, from losing Livvy and Logan, to not passing The Guard, to Tyler, and ending up here.

"What a dirty son of a bitch! He deserves to rot in hell! Who the hell does he think he is to betray you like that? I should destroy him in his dreams!" she squeals.

"Sorry, what?"

"Erm…. Yeah. So, I didn't mean to say that. Please don't tell anyone! They don't know. Please don't tell!" she pleads.

"Rose, are you a dream walker?" I whisper, and she nods, my eyes going wide. The possibilities are endless! We could reach Xander! We could tell him where we are, or she could. We could at least give him an idea!

"Rose, this is amazing!" I squeak.

"What's amazing?" I turn and see Michael at the door, he struts into the room and stands before us.

"Well you, duh!" I say to him in a hope of distracting him.

"Well, obviously! But you don't even know the half of it. Ladies, you are in for a treat today. I got approval from the boss man. We're going outside!"

I jump up and hug him. How he knew I needed this I will never know, but any hard feelings I may have felt towards him melt away in that moment.

"Thank you. Thank you!"

"Oh, that's not the half of it, girlie. You've earned the grand tour," he winks. "You're now allowed to roam as you please."

This day just got a whole lot freaking better! If I'm going to be captive here, at least I'll have the illusion of freedom, and with Rose's newest secret, we could be out of here sooner than I imagined!

DESCENT

Michael walks us through the maze that is Casa de Kaden, but he shows us ways of working out where we are, patterns in the ceiling, codes in the decoration, small things you would never notice if you didn't know they existed.

"Now then, ladies, how about a long drink before we head outside?" Michael says with a flair only he can manage. We both nod and follow him through more corridors, until he brings us back to that dreadful room, where I found Rose. I hear her gasp and she freezes, going paler – if that's even possible.

"Erm, Michael? What are we doing here?" I ask quietly. I don't want to make Rose jump; she looks like she's going to shatter.

"Shit, sorry, honey, I didn't even think. You're safe now, I swear it. All that's beyond here is a bar, and if you listen, it sounds like someone's already playing on the stage," he says, slowly stepping towards Rose until he's upon her, squeezing her into his side. I can see her visibly relax and the relief is real. I hate that she still suffers like this. Her nightmares still haunt her even though they've gotten better.

"Are you guys coming in here or not?" I hear Celeste yell from inside the room. Ugh, I'd like to hope she's not in bitch mode, but I know better. I grab Rose's hand and pull her in, Michael following behind her. I look around the room and it looks completely different. More like a café bar, with a stage area where Celeste is sat at a piano, and then there are tables and chairs scattered around the room. It's so light and airy that if I didn't know better, I'd think it was a completely different room.

"You guys are a little early for cocktails and karaoke," Celeste laughs, and I'm a little lost. It must show on my face because she laughs at me.

"Oh, my God!" Michael exclaims. "Why didn't I think about that! I've been walking them around this mausoleum when we could have been having cocktails and karaoke!" He claps his hands. "Girls, you are in for a treat."

"Erm... not to be the human in the room, but what the hell is karaoke?" I ask. I hate being out of the loop. Michael and Celeste look at me, with a look of wonder on their faces.

"Oh, honey, there is so much we have to teach you!" Michael says, looking at me over his shoulder as he walks over to the bar. He throws around bottles, pouring them into a few big jugs, adding juices and fruit to them before bringing them over to us.

"Drink up, ladies, don't be shy. Now watch and learn," Michael says to us as he pours us each a glass from one of the jugs, before walking over to the stage and pulling a TV screen to the middle, and two microphone stands.

DESCENT

Back in my room, Rose is passed out in bed and I can't help but reflect on how bizarre the day has been.

What I learned today is; cocktails are deliciously lethal, and, karaoke is hilarious. Watching Michael and Celeste become more and more wasted, meaning they got more and more outrageous with their song choices, has been brilliant. After a few dozen cocktails, Rose plucked up the courage to sing, and we were all blown away. After listening to Michael and Celeste burn through the entire catalogue of Wham, Cher and various others, listening to her soft voice was entrancing. She sang a song I've never heard before, a song about being locked away with no-one but your own voices for company. It was so sad, so emotional that I think I even saw Celeste shed a tear.

Then Kaden arrived.

I thought the party was over when he walked in with two of his generals, but it turns out he has a fun side, too. He joined us, apparently whiskey is his drink of choice, and sat drinking with us. I daren't get up and sing; no-one needs to listen to that sort of torture, but then Kaden surprised us. I think Michael and Celeste looked more shocked than I did. He stumbled up to the microphone and the soundtrack to 'Smooth Criminal' started and Michael started laughing. It was infectious and we laughed until we cried, made even worse when he dedicated the song to me singing, 'Addie are you okay?' with the most awful dance moves I have ever seen in my life.

Who would have thought that the dickhead would have a softer, more playful side? It was nice to see but I'm more confused than ever. How could that guy be the one responsible for the horrific things Rose has been through? How could he be the one responsible for killing Livvy? Be responsible for taking me?

I walk over to the bed and lay down, the thoughts buzzing through my head make it hurt. Everything I thought I understood is starting to unravel, and I have no idea which way is up anymore.

DESCENT

Chapter Fourteen

ADDIE

The last few weeks have passed so quickly. My new found freedom has made being here much more bearable. After Michael and Celeste walked me through a few hundred times, I finally got a clue about this place. It's freaking huge, and it really is a maze. It's no surprise that I had no idea of where I was going before. I've barely seen Kaden, and I'm happy about that. Ever since I broke down again in the shower, I've managed to keep my emotions in check and not lose my shit; I'm not sure I'll be able to do that if I see him. I'm still fully confused by him, and I'm not ready to face it all, or make sense of it yet.

Plus, I've been busy focusing on helping Rose contact Xander, but she's had no luck in managing to get to him. Apparently, he doesn't sleep much, or if he is sleeping, it's not when we are. Rose thinks it's her, because she hasn't practiced in so long so we've stopped for a while. I could see how much it was affecting her and she felt like she was letting me down. Plus, we didn't want anyone to question why she was suddenly so tired and sad again.

Since my new found freedom, I've spent a lot of time down in the music bar. There is always live music on here. Michael tells me they're cover bands, covering the music from 'the good old times'. Apparently, I've heard everything; Pink Floyd, U2, Metallica, to someone called Lady Gaga – I mean, what the hell sort of name is that! But I like it down here none the less. The music soothes me. It makes me wish I could play the guitar or the piano. Music was never an option at The Academy. It is only ever the Fae or the Vampyrs who perform.

I signal to Anya for another drink. She's another Vampyr here, but she's always been nice to me. I get the feeling she's not here by choice, but what do I know? She's not from here either, she told me she's from Russia, and from what I remember, that's half a world away, literally. But she's amazing, and I love the way her accent sounds.

"You want another?" she asks me.

"Sure, why not!" I smile. I've grown to like the sweet soda Kaden gave me on my first night here.

"I've got something a little stronger than that, but just as sweet. You should give it a go. Variety is the spice of life, right?" she laughs, walking away and pours me a drink over ice. It is a clear liquid from a clear bottle. She places it in front of me with a smile.

"What is it?" I ask.

"Just drink it, you wouldn't know what it was if I told you." I take a sip of the drink and it burns as it goes down, making my eyes water.

"That, my dear, is the water of my homeland. Vodka. Beautiful. It will keep you strong, but I know you like it sweet, so that was peach vodka," she says proudly. It actually tastes okay once you get over the burning, and I find myself sipping away at it, listening to the music playing as the night slips away.

Oh, my God, my head! I can barely open my eyes. What the hell is this pain? I groan and that's when I hear Michael chuckling beside me.

"Morning, sweetie. Welcome to your first hangover!" he almost sings. I groan as I roll over, trying to bury my head in the pillow mountain, which surrounds me.

"Sorry, not today, honey. Kaden has requested your presence. So you need to get up, so we can feed you and get you to him before he loses his damn mind." He clucks at me, pulling off the comforter and lifting me from the bed.

DESCENT

My head hurts so much that there's little to no resistance from me, and then I'm falling. Water splashes around me. That dick dropped me in the bath! I look up at him in stupor.

"At least it's warm," I grumble. I wait for him to leave the room, then strip off my wet clothes and bathe. I get myself to a presentable state and tell Michael I'm ready to go.

"Food first, cupcake."

"I don't know if I can eat," I say. My stomach is swirling from the lack of food I ate yesterday, and the amount of vodka I drank. In my defence, it tasted good – so good. I follow him down to the dining room and make my way over to the breakfast buffet. Suddenly, the thought of grease makes me ravenous, so I grab a plate and load it up with bacon, scrambled eggs, hash browns, with a side of blueberry pancakes. The only good thing about here is the food. I head over to an empty table and sit before diving into my food. Rose and Michael join me, both with much less food than me. They look at me like I've lost my mind.

"Fuck it, ya know?" I smile. "You only live once, and people are going to judge anyway, so I say be happy and eat free."

Michael laughs and starts eating his breakfast, while Rose picks at hers, just staring at me in wonder.

We finish breakfast and I head back to the music room, where Michael has informed me Kaden is waiting. They have gone out to the lake for a boat ride. I want to go on a boat, dammit, not talk to this asshat!

Kaden is sat at a table in front of the stage. It's not hard to spot him, he's the only person in here other than Anya who is behind the bar again. She winks at me and I wave hello, before making my way across the room to Kaden.

"You summoned me, oh mighty one," I say.

The look on his face is terse, and I start to worry about what I'm doing here.

"Sit down, Addie. We need to talk."

I take a seat opposite him as Anya appears with a glass for us each. I take a sip, thankful it's only soda. I don't think I could handle anything stronger right now, though from the look on Kaden's face, I might need it.

"What do you know about my kind, Addie?" he asks looking tense.

"I know what I was taught; Vampyrs are almost as old as the Fae, though no-one seems to know how the first Vampyrs came to be, they've been on earth more than a few lifetimes over. I know that to become a Vampyr, you can either be born, though it is rare, or you can be turned by the head of a syreline, but it is a long and painful process. I know you need human blood to survive, but can eat and drink the same things I do, too – and that you

211

thrive when you do. I've also heard that alcohol helps curb the blood lust for some Vampyrs. Should I keep going?"

"Yes."

"Okay, um, I know you're stronger and faster than humans, though some Fae can move faster and can be stronger than you, dependant on their blood lines. I know you were divided by The Dark War, and where before there were thirteen houses who lived reasonably harmoniously, five of the houses joined the Demon King, and the rest joined the Fae. I know most of the Vampyrs who joined the Demon King, the lesser Vampyrs, the newer ones became Shades, they lost their humanity fighting for the Demon King because he fed on their souls. Honestly, I think that's about everything. Why are you asking?"

"I'm asking, Addie, because you've been lied to. All of you have been lied to for years, and it angers me. We hid for so long before the war because everyone thought the world would implode if the humans knew about the supernatural world, but there is no excuse anymore. Humans have accepted Vampyrs and Fae and so lying to them, or giving them false truths just seems insane. Don't you agree?" he asks, but I get the feeling he's not really asking me a question so I just nod and let him keep talking with no idea what he's going on about.

"The Fae know exactly what the origins of the Vampyrs are, hell, they helped make us."

"I'm sorry, what? They made you? But how?" I ask. I don't understand why no one ever told us.

"Yes, they helped make us. I guess I need to go further back, to where we came from in the first place. The original Vampyrs, those of us like me, Xander, Dimitri, Michael and Celeste, and others. We are what is now known as The Fallen, but once, once we were Angels."

"I'm sorry, what?! Angels? I didn't think they existed. We were taught Angels and God were a myth, taught by ignorant humans from the start of days to give them something bigger than themselves to believe in."

"Of course you were; that's what they wanted you to think. I can't tell you much about God – I sure as hell never saw him. All I knew was Cole was our leader, and when the end of our world as we knew it came to an end, we had two choices; perish alongside our brothers and sisters, who clung to the world we loved as it was destroyed, or Fall. Many of us fell, but once here, we found we were no longer as strong, and we started to weaken rapidly. Many of my family died before the Fae found us and helped. Their earth magic mixed with royal Fae blood restored us; we flourished; our wings became strong again. What they didn't tell us about was the blood lust, our dependency on human blood to survive. Some accepted their new dependency, while others despised the Fae for not telling the whole truth. As you can see, it's a flaw they constantly flaunt."

213

DESCENT

"I'm sorry, did you say wings?" I gasp

"From all that, all you got was wings?" he sighs.

"No obviously not, but honestly, it sounds like a twisted fairy tale. It's just more than a little unbelievable."

He stands, shrugging off his jacket and then taking off his long sleeved tee. Soon he is standing before me barefoot, in just black jeans. I can't help but once again admire him. He is covered in tattoos. I hadn't noticed them before, but they're everywhere. The images go down both his arms, with writing across his chest and collarbones. *'Fortitudo Aedificat Moribus'*. It's some form of old language, Latin I think, but I'm not positive. They trail down his chest and abs, dipping below his trouser line. He's just so pretty to look at that it's a shame he's such an ass, a delusional one, too from the sounds of it.

"You don't believe me, do you?" he asks with a smirk on his face.

"Not entirely, no."

"I had a feeling…"

He stretches his neck and closes his eyes, and I hear what sounds like bones crunching, followed by a whoosh.

"Holy fuck…." *HE HAS FREAKING WINGS!* Huge black feathered wings, the tips of each feather turning to grey. They're beautiful. I think I'm in shock. I step toward him with my hand stretched out in front of me, but stop just before I touch them. I look at him, asking permission, and he nods. I move forward with wide eyes and stroke the

214

feathers of his wings. He moans softly, but I can't stop touching them. I'm mesmerised. They're so soft, layered in such a way that they hide the strength they hold. I press my hand against them, and I can feel the taut muscle beneath the soft exterior.

"Believe me now?" he asks, his voice tight. I pull my hand back and look at him with wide eyes.

"How can I not? This is... amazing! I just don't understand why you hide?"

"Because the Fae bound us, they swore us to secrecy – we could never tell any human."

"So why tell me? Why risk it?"

"You'll see in time. Would you like to fly, Addie?"

I shake my head. This is amazing, but I still don't trust him, even if he is the only person to ever tell me the truth.

"No? Maybe next time." He smirks, before folding his wings away. He turns around once they're gone, and there is no trace of them, his back is smooth and lean. He puts his top back on and turns to face me.

"I imagine this is a lot to take in. Do you have anything you want to ask me?"

I sit down staring at him, gawping almost. I have no freaking idea what is going on. I pinch my arm, *ouch*, nope, I'm awake.

"I guess not; you took this much better than I thought you would. Maybe it's the shock. I've got some things I need to attend to, but I'm sure you see why we needed to talk. I will see you soon, Addie."

I sit at the table reeling. I don't want to believe him. I don't want to trust him, but the look on his face... I just know he wasn't lying to me. Hell, he showed me the truth; he stood there and revealed himself to me, and now I have no idea what to do. I don't understand why this has been kept from everyone. Surely this would give them something more to believe in, something bigger? Maybe that's why. And then... then there's Xander and Dimitri. They lied to me, too. I don't know which one hurts more, Xander because of how close we've become, or Dimitri who's known me my entire life. Do I even really know them at all? I don't know whether or not to be angry at them or disappointed they didn't trust me enough. Hell Kaden did! Plus, I'm still here, and there's no sign anyone is coming for me. After all this time, I've lost any hope I had of them finding me, or of Rose being able to contact them. Maybe I don't mean as much to them as I thought.

I sway to the music coming from the girl on the stage. I swear live music is the only constant in this place. Her words call to me,

"Don't speak, I can't believe this here is happening, our situation isn't right… What if I need you to save me? Would you even try? Or would you find some lame excuse to never be true?"

Her words resonate; she sounds so sad but strong all at the same time. I recognise her but I don't know where from. I signal for another drink from the one of the other guys behind the bar, and he puts another drink in front of me. Who would've thought something as girlie as peach vodka would be my drink of choice? I take a sip and thank Anya silently for introducing me to it. I focus on the burn as it goes down, to avoid thinking about my world burning down around me. I mean, I might be exaggerating but after the way Ty lied to me, I've had enough of non-truths. Even if they're just omissions of the truth, it's still a lie. He had freaking wings! Huge black feathered wings, and apparently all the originals have them. I'm not sure how to process it. I finish my drink and head back to my 'room'.

The only good thing about having been here for so long is that I finally know my way around – for the most part at least. And that means my chance of escape is better – that's my plan of action. I get to my room and see Rose sat on my bed, listening to music from the new toy Kaden gave to me via Michael. It's so small, but it plays music and has headphones so I can block out the world. I'm so glad she's finally comfortable around me, even if she won't leave the room without me or Michael, and trembles every time one of the others comes near. Though, after what Kaden told me, maybe that's not so strange after all.

Knowing that those original twenty are still the way they are because of royal Fae blood, and with her being a royal Fae puts her in a very difficult situation.

"Hey, Rose, are you okay?" I ask sitting next to her on the bed.

"I am, thank you. Are you?"

"Erm, I think so, considering everything."

"I'm just so grateful to you for helping me. I can't ask for anything more. My life has been one tragedy after another; left for dead as a child and then found by these monsters after hiding for so long. I think you might be the first person to ever be truly kind to me. My first friend," she says wistfully, staring out across the water through the window. My heart breaks for her all over again. She hasn't spoken much about what happened to her before. She's so sweet, so innocent and pure, she doesn't deserve the hand fate has dealt her.

"Rose, can I ask you a question?"

She looks at me with caution in her eyes but nods.

"Did you know about Kaden? About him, Michael and Celeste? About Xander, and what they really are?" Her eyes go wide with fear, and I know she knows, but she also knows I shouldn't know.

"Don't worry," I reassure her. "It was Kaden who told me, well showed me really, so you don't have to worry about people thinking you told me. You're safe with me. Always, okay?" The panic inside her ebbs and she nods again. Then her arms are around me, hugging me.

"Thank you, Addie. I think I might be dead by now if it wasn't for you. I don't think I would have survived another night of their games."

"You're stronger than you know, Rose. You'd have made it through. You survived so much before I came along. You'd have saved yourself if I hadn't been here," I say, hugging her back.

I know she doesn't believe me. A knock on the door causes her to go instantly rigid.

"It will be fine; I promise," I whisper. The door opens and Michael enters the room with his usual flair.

"Hello, beautifuls. I am to be your dashing escort this afternoon," he says with a smile.

"Dude, do you ever wear a shirt?" I ask, teasing him.

"Sweetie, why the hell would I cover this up? I mean, look at me. Really! Cover up? Ha!"

I can't help but laugh.

"And where exactly is it you're whisking us away to, my dashing prince?" I ask. I can't hold what I now know against him. He's been the one person here who has been nothing but nice to me, more than nice, he's the only person here I'd consider an actual friend.

DESCENT

"Well, sweetie; that's where the sad part comes, for me anyway," he says.

I scrutinise his face – suddenly alarmed. I stand, ready to fight.

"Come on, Michael, spit it out. Where are we going?"

"Home, Addie. I'm taking you home."

"WHAT?" I shout. This must be some sort of trick. Surely after everything, they're not just going to let me go?

"That's exactly why it's me taking you home. I fought with Kaden about it, but I knew you'd need to hear this from me. Trust me, Addie. I wouldn't lie to you. I've never lied to you about a thing. It was me who pushed him to tell you. I've been pushing him since the day you got here. You're going home, and Rose gets to go with you. You can thank me for that little bit, too."

I'm frozen. I have no idea what I'm meant to say or do here. I mean, I'm happy to be going home. But why? Why now? After Tyler's betrayal I can't entirely trust anyone again. Rose rushes past me and throws herself around Michael. I can't help but feel suspicion and unease. It makes no sense.

"Thank you, thank you, thank you!" she says, hugging him and crying. I smile as he embraces her gently. I guess in the time he spent with us, he realised just how much she needed this. I nod and look around me. I think I might miss this place, just a tiny bit.

"What happens now? When do we leave? Why do we get to go?" I ask.

"Come on, Ads, you know I can't tell you all of that. Just know that I'm taking you home – like right now so grab anything you want or need, Kaden will have anything left here brought to you, probably by me, later. You, too, Rose."

I'm already dressed so I grab the leather jacket I've been wearing while I've been here and I'm ready. Rose grabs some shoes from my closet and a long white cloak before announcing she's ready.

Michael looks us both over, making sure we're ready before looking at me sadly. "Let's go."

DESCENT

ADDIE

Michael soars above us, and I see The Academy in the distance out the window of the car that has been provided for us. I've never been in one of these before, well not whilst conscious. I understand why people in the Old World were crazy about them. We've been travelling for about four days now, and my butt hasn't fallen asleep once on this chair. Rose is in the back seat; she's practically bouncing back there at the prospect of being free.

I look at Celeste who is driving us home. Her and Michael have taken turns between flying and driving. Considering no-one is meant to know about them and their wings, they've not exactly hidden them on this journey.

Michael said it was so they had better sight to scout the road ahead, explaining that the roads aren't always safe, especially for humans. Who would attack us is beyond me. Surely the Shades are the biggest threat out here, and they're under Kaden's command. I didn't bother asking, knowing I wouldn't get an answer.

I don't know how I feel about going back. Obviously, I'm happy to be home, but is this really home anymore? Especially now I know everyone lied to me, and with Michael up there, they're going to know I know their big secret. The anxiety claws at me. I have no idea what happened to Tyler or if he's even still here. They might not even know he had anything to do with my abduction. I have no idea what to expect, and it feels like it's been so long. Three months is nothing in the grand scheme of things, but to me, it's felt like an eternity. The Academy will probably be prepping for graduation; everyone about to start their new lives, and I have no idea what I'll even do. My life long goal has been the guard, and Xander crushed that dream when he rejected me from the guard. I haven't even had chance to think about that until now. So much has taken precedent. Holy crap, what am I going to do!

I take a few deep breaths to calm myself, as we near the Academy gates I can see Xander and Dimitri, along with other Vampyrs... I mean Fallen... I mean... Oh I don't even know! They're stood in line, with Xander in the middle, Dimitri to his right and a huge, dark skinned man to his left. They look ready for battle, like the warriors that they are. Do they know it's us? We draw to a stop about twenty feet from Xander and Michael lands in front of the car, his wings spread to full span. They match his amazing electric blue hair, they're blue tipped with green, they're so freaking awesome! He stays down on one knee with his head tilted to the floor for a minute, before standing, leaving his wings on show. He turns to me and winks, with a reassuring smile, motioning for me to get out.

"Are you ready Rose? Cause this is it."

"I don't think I've ever been more ready for anything in my entire life!" she squeals excitedly. I look to Celeste who nods and opens her door at the same time I open mine. I wait for Rose to exit the car before moving around Michael's wings, which have been hiding us from sight.

"Addie? Is that you?" I hear Dimitri call over, I know he can see it's me, and I haven't changed that much. Sure my hairs a little longer, and I'm not as lean as I was as I've not been able to train, but I'm not that different. He starts to approach us, but Xander stops him.

"Michael, Celeste. What are you doing here?" Xander asks. He barely raises his voice, knowing that they'll be able to hear even if he whispers.

"We've come to return our friend home, Xander," Michael replies. "I thought you'd be happy to see her."

Xander's face is hard, emotionless. "Well, thank you for bringing her home, and the other one?"

"Are you freaking kidding me?!" I shout. "I've been gone for three god damn months. You have no idea where I've been, what has happened, and yet you talk about me as if I'm not standing here. I don't fucking think so." I turn to Celeste and Michael, "Thank you both so much for getting me home safely."

Celeste nods and gets back in the car, whilst Michael swoops me up in a hug.

"Thank you for everything, Mikey. I don't know what I'd have done without you," I whisper as I hug him back.

"Anytime, baby doll. Don't you be a stranger, you hear? You ever need me and I'll be there. I'll make sure you can get in touch with me," he says fiercely before letting me go.

I wipe away the tears, which threaten to spill down my face. He hugs Rose then heads to the car and I blow him a kiss as he climbs in. He starts the car, reverses out and then drives away. When I can't see them anymore, I turn back to face Xander and his merry band of warriors.

"So, Mr Bane, have I passed your test yet? Are you going to allow me back into The Academy? Are you going to explain to me about why you've all been lying to me? Lying to all of the human race about what you really are? Oh and my friend here is Rose Frostheart, you might recognise her name."

I see faces pale at my words, especially with the introduction of Rose, but they remain warriors through it all, barely letting it show.

"Did you say Frostheart? As in the Royal Fae family from the Isles?"

Rose is still partially hidden by me, hiding, and I don't blame her. She thought this would be a welcoming party, not a line-up of elite, looking over at us with suspicion.

"You're damn straight. Now, will you move out of my god damn way and let us in so I can make sure she's okay? She's been through enough without you freaking brutes staring her down like the enemy without even speaking to her."

With that, each one of them falls to one knee and bows their head, their fists closed over their hearts. I'm amazed. It turns out Fae royalty get, well, the royal treatment. Xander lifts his head and looks behind me.

"Apologies, your highness. It has been so very long since I saw you that I did not recognise you. I understood you to be dead. Please forgive my mistake, and forgive our behaviour."

Rose steps beside me, still clinging to my arm.

"You are forgiven, Xander Bane, as are the rest of what I assume are your Elite. Please stand, I have not been knelt to in such a long time. You are probably right to have assumed me dead; I have been missing from Fae court for far too long, I feared my family thought the worst. I can see now I was right." She squeezes my hand and I know she can't handle much more of this right now.

"Xander," I say. "Please can we just come in and talk later. We've been travelling for days Just let us go back to my room and rest, and we can go through everything tomorrow. Please."

Dimitri stalks forward and wraps me up in a hug, lifting me off the floor.

"Dimitri... I still need to breathe," I wheeze out.

"Sorry, Addie but I missed you. I was so worried. I should have known better. Ignore him; he's just pissed he didn't get to rescue you. Let's get you both inside. Rose, we have quarters for the Royals who stay with us, we can put you up there, whilst Addie goes back to her dorm room.

I feel Rose flinch. "Not a chance Dimitri," I say. "You have no idea what we've both been through, what Rose has been through. She can't sleep alone. She's with me or I'm with her, that's the deal."

Dimitri casts a glance at Rose and on seeing her small nod, says "Okay, Addie, we'll put you both in the Royal quarters for now. Saves the scrutiny and questions for you from the other students here too, let's go."

He walks back towards Xander, and the Elite are now at ease. Some walk ahead of us through the gates, the rest fall behind us.

They lead us to our rooms before leaving us alone for a few hours. I'm helping Rose get settled in when Dimitri knocks on the door.

"Hey, Addie, you got a minute?" he asks, smiling. I have really missed him, and no matter how angry I am at him, that doesn't diminish the relief of seeing him. I get up and run to him, wrapping my arms around him. He's shocked, I can feel it, but he relaxes after a second and hugs me back.

"I'm glad your back," he says quietly.

"Me too Dimitri, me too. I was beginning to think I'd never see you guys again."

"I'd never have let that happen, Addie – and neither would Xander. He's been a riot since you were taken." He rolls his eyes, making me laugh. "Anyway, we need to speak to you before the Eight arrive. Can you come now?"

I look at Rose and she nods and smiles at me. "I'll be fine, Addie, I swear. Go! They need to know what happened."

I give her a small hug before following Dimitri out of the room and into the guards' quarters. I knew the Elite were staying here. I guess this is where they've been hiding. He leads me into a room with a long table, around which the Elite are sat with Xander at the head. The seat to his right is free and I assume that is for Dimitri. Look around the rest of the Elite, I recognise some but not others. Dimitri leads me to the seat at the tail of the table. I sit down and the silence of the room washes over me as I watch Dimitri take his seat.

"Addie," Xander addresses me coldly, his hands joined beneath his chin, "Before we get started, let me officially introduce you my Elite. You already know Dimitri, next to him is; Zero, Rome, Salene, and over there is Gunner, Lex, Bray and Aliana."

They each nod or smile at me as they are introduced.

"Some of them fought for you when you were taken, and we were all searching for you in the months you were gone. I thought it important everyone be present to hear your testimony."

They question me for what feels like hours but I know this is nothing compared to what it will be like when the Eight arrive. I answer everything as best I can, with none of my questions being answered, like 'Do you guys all have wings, too?' As I explain to them all what we actually went through, I could see Xander's hard exterior softening. It's nice to see that he still cares. Things have been so rollercoaster with us, it's hard to keep up.

Xander watches me like precious cargo the entire time, like he's worried if he looks away I'll disappear again. When they seem satisfied, the Elite leave the room, leaving me alone with Xander. He walks over to me and perches on the table in front of me.

"Are you really okay, Addie?" he asks, brushing some hair off my face and tucking it behind my ear. His touch is so soft, and he looks at me like I'm the moon and the stars. I reach up and touch his hand, this is the first time I register that he might actually like me in *that* way. I know we ran together before.... but....

"I'm fine, I swear. I didn't lie – they were surprisingly nice to me. Even Kaden."

He flinches at the name.

"He said you guys had history, but he didn't really elaborate on it much – or on much really, other than you know, the fact you're Fallen and have wings!"

He flinches again and I think, *Okay, so I totally didn't mean to throw that bit in*

"I know I'm not meant to know about it," I say hurriedly, "but will you talk to me about it? Knowing about it but not being able to talk about it is almost impossible, and I don't want to get anyone into trouble by talking to people I'm not meant to."

"Addie, breath!" he laughs. "You're adorable when you ramble on. Yes, I'll speak to you about it, but you can't let anyone else know that you know the truth. My Elite are the exception; they are loyal to me, and therefore, loyal to you, but not everyone will be happy about you knowing. What did Kaden tell you?"

I get up and sit on the floor and he looks at me like I've lost my mind, but those seats really aren't that comfortable. He follows my lead and sits, leaning against a wall. I go through the entire conversation I had with Kaden, including when he revealed his wings to me. I leave out the bit about touching them; I get the feeling that's not something he'd want to hear.

"I'm amazed you took all of this so well, Addie. You've been through so much, then to find out that what you thought you were fighting for from the beginning wasn't the real truth, you're surprisingly calm."

"Oh, I'm not calm, but what good would it do me unleashing the hell that's inside me on you? It sure as shit wouldn't make you talk to me, that much I know."

"I think I could forgive you almost anything, Addie," he whispers. I don't know what to say to that so I say nothing, and we sit in a comfortable silence, digesting everything.

"So you and Kaden were close, huh?" I ask. The question has been eating at me since I saw him flinch earlier. A nicer person wouldn't bring it up, but I have an unquenchable need to know everything about him that I can.

"You could say that. Kaden is my brother."

"Sorry, what? Your brother, as in actual brother? How is that even possible?"

He chuckles and wraps his arm around my shoulders, pulling me close to him. I don't think he even realises he's doing it until I'm pressed against him. *Wow he smells good.*

"The same way you or any other would have a brother or sister, Addie. Before we fell, our lives, in general, were very much the same as humans. You know, other than the obvious differences. Our parents were both warriors, which is how we both rose to such high stations at such a young age."

I raise an eyebrow at him. "Young? Ha!"

"Age is relative; it was young for Angels at least. Anyway, once we fell, and everything with the Fae happened, Kaden became bitter. The old Kaden was still there, buried deep inside him, but Cole, our old General, plagued his mind. He relied on the anger and betrayal Kaden felt, and turned him against the Fae. Against me." His head drops, and I can tell the pain has not healed.

"It was a long time ago, but knowing he was so good to you, makes me believe the Kaden I knew is still inside him somewhere. The Kaden who captured Rose – that's the new Kaden. I feel responsible for him and every action he makes. He's my little brother; I should have been there for him more. I should have done more."

I can feel his pain. It radiates of him in waves and it's excruciating. I turn my face to his. We're so close that I can feel his breath on my face. I can almost taste his kiss. His hand strokes my waist, and before I know it, he's pulled me onto his lap so we are face to face, his hands cupping my ass, he closes the distance between us.

The feeling of his lips on mine is overwhelming. There are so many silent demands in his kiss and yet, such gentleness that it's a whirlwind. I pull back to catch my breath. He stands, lifting me with him easily, never breaking eye contact.

"More…" I breathe and he captures my lips again. He pushes me back against the wall, entwining his fingers with mine, pinning me to the wall. Instinctively, I arch into him and I swear I hear him growl. The noise sends waves south; every nerve ending on edge. I need more of him. I free my hands, tightening my arms around his neck, wrapping my legs tight around his waist to steady myself, pushing my hips against his. He relents, releasing me. I run my hands up his back, feeling every tense muscle. The strength and power of him excites me further, and I push deeper into his kiss, forcing my fingers through his soft and silky hair.

A cough interrupts us and it's my turn to growl. *Dammit!* I look up and see Dimitri smirking at me from the doorway. *Holy shit.* Xander still hasn't moved, and from what I can feel, he's not likely to anytime soon.

"What?" he barks, not even looking a Dimitri, his face buried in my neck.

"You're needed outside. The rest of the Eight have just arrived."

"They always did have impeccable timing," he bites out. I swallow the laugh which bubbles up. I can feel the heat in my face as I try to look anywhere but at Dimitri.

"I'll be down shortly."

"I'll let them know," he says. "Addie." He waves to me as he leaves and I let my head drop to Xander's shoulder.

"To be continued?" I ask, and he moans.

"That, you can count on."

It's been a week since we got back to The Academy, and I swear if I get asked one more question, I'm going to break someone. What part of 'I have no idea' don't these people understand? I can only say it so many ways. No I don't know why he took me. No I don't know where I was. No I don't know why he brought me back. I must sound like a dim-witted idiot, but I know nothing. Needless to say, there were fireworks. And lots of things were thrown, albeit not all by me. Though, I have let them have it in full about lying to me and everyone.

After being cooped up for so long, I'm itching to go running and train again, but Xander has Rose and I pretty much on lockdown. Today, I'm going outside whether he wants me to or not. Today is Graduation. Today I get to see Benny and find out what happened after I left. I already know no one has seen Tyler since the night I was taken, and no one seems to know what happened to him.

I put on my training gear with the intention of sneaking out. I'm so excited about seeing Benny again. There's no-one else still on campus and it feels that somehow my disappearance permanently ended something. Benny knows me, he knew me before all of the crazy, and I didn't realise how much I needed that until just now.

Outside at last! I stretch out and start across the green. The wind against my face and the burn in my calves never felt so good! I feel my body start to relax back into the rhythm, happy to be moving freely again. I run until I can't run anymore. I come to a stop and fall to the floor, spread out on my back, I relish the burn of my lungs with each breath. Then I realise where I am and the breath leaves me. I'm at our tree. The one where I said goodbye. The one where Xander first held me. The rush of emotions causes a physical painful. I need to get up and run again.

"Is that you, Short Stack?" I hear yelled across the green. I look up to see Benny coming towards me. I'm up on my feet, running towards him and bundling into him.

"Hey you," he says. "I missed you! I'm so glad you're okay!" he hugs me tightly. Tears prick my eyes and I squeeze them shut to hold them back, hugging him a bit tighter.

"I missed you too, Benny!" I laugh, "I never thought I'd say that."

He laughs and it shakes his body. He puts me down and tucks me under his arm.

"Come on, Short Stack. We need to go get a drink!"

"Hell, yes! I knew missing you was a good thing," I giggle and follow him back to his dorm room. He tells me about things I've missed since I've been gone, the things I wasn't debriefed about by Xander. Apparently, not much has changed since I left. I mean, sure most of my year have moved on, but other than that, nothing.

"What about you, Addie? What happened when you were gone?"

I look at him and I can see the concern in his eyes. There's no judgment, no curiosity, just concern.

"I'm okay, Benny. Nothing bad really happened. Yes, I was taken, but I had a nice room, no-one hurt me. I was yelled at a few times but I don't think they wanted to hurt me; they just wanted to tell me some stuff, see if what I knew was real. Actually, some of them were nice people, ya know. It's pretty surreal. Everyone keeps telling me that they're the bad guys, but they weren't. Not to me, anyway. I know they've done and still do, bad things, hell Rose can confirm that, but they're not all bad."

He shakes his head.

"Only you could see the upside of being kidnapped. I guess Livvy left more of her in you than we realised. You seem okay so I guess I'll have to believe that you're really okay. Now who is this Rose I've heard so much about?" He smirks and I slap him upside the head.

"You never change, do you, Benny?" I laugh. "Anyway, you better take me back to the Royal quarters before they send out a search party – or not."

Benny looks at me, serious. "They did look for you. They did care, you know." He's grown up a lot since I saw him last. I know he's still a joker, but you can see it in his eyes. They're older, he's seen more, lived through more and not all good. His new found maturity suits him.

I roll my eyes and smile sadly. "Come on. Time to take me back to my princess rooms."

"Really Addie?" he groans.

"This way, I can introduce to you Rose." I wink at him and jump up. We head back to the Royal quarters to be met by a very angry Xander and Dimitri. Rose is crying with all the tension and I immediately bristle.

"What the hell did you do to her?" I ask, moving over to her and hugging her. Benny follows me, the anger rippling through him is evident in his giant frame. He stands between us and them, rigid, standing guard.

"Us?" Xander bites, "You're the one who left her on her own. We came looking for you and she didn't know where you were!"

"So what? You interrogated her? Don't you think she's been through enough? And there was me thinking you both knew me well enough to know I'd never stay locked up in this fucking tower." I hand Rose over to Benny and charge towards the others, my hands on my hips and my cheeks sucked "Could you two be any more fucking stupid? Did you forget who she is?"

It's clear they realise they messed up.

"Sorry," Dimitri mumbles. I look to Xander who is unable to make eye contact. I can see the knot of muscle in his jaw as he tries to contain his anger.

"It's not me you need to say sorry to," I say nodding in the direction of Rose, but it seems Benny has worked his magic because she's already smiling and blushing. I grab a drink from the fridge trying to calm my anger. I know that they were partly right – I did leave her alone. I put my own wants first.

"So why are you here, exactly," I snap.

Xander leaves Dimitri to speak, he's still too busy chewing a wasp. "We came here to tell you the Valoires have invited Rose to join them at the palace. The Frosthearts have been contacted and they are coming to take her home, but as they have so far to travel and so much to prepare, they've asked she stay with the Valoires until they can get here."

"What?" Rose squeaks. "I don't want to go. Addie, please don't make me go. I can't go away again. Not on my own. Please, please don't make me go," she begs. Benny holds her up as she starts to panic. I grab her hands and look her in her eyes.

"It's going to be okay. I've got you. Remember, I told you, I won't let anything bad happen to you again." She visibly relaxes and Benny whispers reassurances to her. The effect he has on her is curious.

"Okay," she says. "I'll go, but Addie and Benny have to come with me." She blushes as she says it, and I can see Benny biting down a smirk – the boy works quick, I'll give him that.

Xander looks less than pleased, but she's a Princess so he can't exactly say no.

"Fine," he groans, running his hand over his face. I'm not exactly ecstatic about it myself; I was looking forward to finally getting back to a normal life. Graduating, getting a life. Normality.

"Come on, Benny, let's go get me graduated so we can get out of this place!"

Graduation was exactly what I expected it to be, we put on the crazy gown and cap, collected a piece of paper to say we'd passed our class, and it also stated what our new role in life would be. Except, mine was blank. Apparently no-one knows what to do with me. Just fucking awesome!

Benny, Lucas and Marc all made sure I was never alone but I couldn't help but notice the absence of Logan and Livvy. All of those we lost were given a black star, which is now on the back wall of the Academy; a memorial for all of those who have been lost over the eons. I noted the vast space just waiting for our own stars, for all those who will be lost going forward. It's a horrific realisation, but the truth is rarely pretty.

Xander gave out the diplomas alongside Marcus DeLauter. As the two leading houses in this territory, it was only fitting that they did it. The Valoire Royals were present, too. They stayed silent in their thrones at the back, centre of the stage. I was struck again by the beauty of the Queen, but it was the first time I had ever seen the King, and the distaste and revulsion he projected was loud and clear. He didn't want to be there.

Once the ceremony was over, people went their own way, though most people ended up back at Benny's for one last party. I tried to get Rose to come along, but I think there were just too many people for her to face. I didn't stay long; it didn't feel right after everything that had passed. I saw Peter as I was leaving, and he apologised for his outburst at our last meeting. He seems better, and I'm glad. He should be able to move forward and be happy.

Now, I'm here in bed, wondering what tomorrow will bring. Going to the Fae palace is my next step, but where do I go from there?

DESCENT

ADDIE

I've been in this car for about two hours, and I'm already itching to get out. I've been inside small spaces far too much recently. We finally pull off the main road, and after about ten minutes, we come to the guard gate. The walls must be at least twelve feet tall. Even Benny is going to have trouble jumping those. I look over at him and see Rose is curled into him, fast asleep. He's out cold, too with his head resting on hers. I'm glad she feels safe around Benny, he's a good guy, and he qualified for the guard, so he's more than capable of looking out for her. Just knowing I'm not the only one with her best interest at heart, lifts a massive weight from me.

Xander and Dimitri have been silent the entire journey. I think Xander is still a little pissed Benny and I are here, and Dimitri, well he knows better than to go against Xander, especially when he's like this.

DESCENT

At the gate, they do their thing with the guards, who eventually let us through the gates. The road to the palace is long and winding. When we finally arrive, I can't see both ends at the same time. I don't think I've ever seen a building so big!

I reach over and shake Rose and Benny awake. She blushes when she realises how close she is to Benny.

"We're here, Rose. Are you ready?" I ask. She's been so nervous about being back around the Fae.

"I think so," she says smoothing down her hair. "I guess we'll see, huh?" she squeaks. Her hands are slightly shaking.

"It's going to be okay. I promise."

I get Rose settled in, and wait with her until she's calmed enough to go to sleep before heading down to find Xander and Dimitri. I ask one of the guard who escorts me to one of the best equipped training rooms I've ever seen. I look around the room in awe, it's amazing.

"Addie, are you okay?" Turning I see Dimitri stood in the doorway.

"Yeah, I'm okay. Just… wow."

"I know, right. But are you really okay? I can't even imagine how you're coping with everything that's happened recently."

"No, I'm not okay," I sigh. "But I will be, I just need to get back to who I am. Get back to normal."

"Well, I'm not sure what sort of normal I can offer, but how about a little piece of the past?" he walks past me and goes into a room behind me before reappearing and handing me a box. *My Sai* It's felt like I've been missing a part of me. Opening the box and lifting them out, feeling the balance of the blade, it's like I'm me again.

"It's good to see you with those again," Xander says from behind me. Looking over at him I can't help the breath that hitches, or how my pulse races. He makes everything in me feel like I'm losing a control, but like it's safe to do so. Like I can be me.

"I have a new play mate for you," he chuckles. "Addie, meet Aliana. You might have met briefly before, but she's going to be in charge of your training until further notice. Aliana steps forward and looks me up and down.

"I'm sure we can get you back in shape," she taunts. I look over at Xander and he's trying to stop a smile, but I can see the struggle.

"Oh we'll see." I grip my Sai tight, the excitement of touching them again, using them, it's more than I can imagine.

"Let's see what you've got to *teach* me shall we?" I know I sound like a cocky bitch, but half this game is self-belief. I'm probably about to get my ass handed to me, but I'm not going to let her know that. She walks over to the weapons hanging on the wall and pulls down a Katana, following me to the middle of the room to the mats. I take my starting stance and call her out.

Oh my life. She threw me around the training room like I was nothing, and as I lie here on my back, winded, staring up at the fans on the ceiling I realise just how out of shape I really am. I try not to dwell on how much I've slipped while I been away, and I fight the tears of frustration that try to claw to the surface. She's a fully trained member of Xander's Elite. Of course, she was going to win, but logic has no place in my train of thought right now. Emotion is ruling me, and I hate that I was humiliated so thoroughly. Dimitri and Aliana left shortly after Xander ended my training session, and I've just laid here since. Pity party for one.

"Do you have plans for tonight?" Xander asks me, coming to lay on the floor beside me.

"You mean other than hiding my humiliation in a ton of junk food. No, nothing. Why?"

"You have no reason to be humiliated, Addie. You fought well. Aliana is one of my best fighters. She's small, so people underestimate her. Exactly how you did, but that's exactly why I picked her to train you. You've fought with me and Dimitri, you know how we fight. Aliana will help you expand your skills. She will make you better."

"While your words make total sense logically, you understand that underneath it all I'm still just a girl right?"

He looks at me like I've lost my mind. "I'm confused."

"Of course you are, you're a guy. I don't want to hear how I have no reason not to be humiliated. I want you to hug me, tell me everything's okay, and just let me feel like crap for a little while. Let me exhaust the crazy emotion train out before handing me the logic. I know what you're saying makes sense, I'm just not ready to hear it yet okay?"

"Okay," he says rolling me into the crook of shoulder, running his hand up and down my arm. Kissing me on top of my head gently, he squeezes me and just holds me and it feels perfect.

XANDER

Today was hard for Addie, I could see that, I'm not stupid, and I've missed her like crazy, so I've told everyone to leave us alone for the night. I want some time with her, especially since I have some news I know she's not going to like.

I know the time is coming upon us quickly when I'm going to have to tell her the truth. I'm just so concerned about how she's going to react. What if she pushes me away? She trusts me now, and I don't want to be just another person who keeps letting her down and betraying her. I've always been a man of my word, which is what makes this so hard. To tell her the truth, I have to break an oath. I have to decide which matters most, and my heart says it's her. She is the most important thing. I'd pick her over everything.

I've reserved the movie room for tonight. It's set up with the best equipment we could get our hands on; from before The Outbreak. A wall-size screen with projector, and leather sofas to stretch out on. One advantage of having been around her for so long, watching from a distance, is I know the small things, like her favourite movie. Don't get me wrong, I shut out everyone, almost all of the time, but it comes in handy when I'm trying to make her happy. I've asked Dimitri to go and get her, to bring her to me blindfolded so she has no idea what's going on. I know she trusts Dimitri, almost above all others.

I hear them coming down the corridor and listen to her laugh as she trips and stumbles. My heart soars at the sound of her happiness. Her laugh is one of my favourite things about her – and she doesn't do it enough.

"Where on earth are you taking me Dimitri? I've really had enough of blindfolds," she sighs

"Addie, I think of you like my little sister, trust me when I say you're safe with me," he reassures her, but I can't help the growl that slips out. Mine.

"Oh, come on Dimitri. Can we take this stupid blindfold off yet? Pleaseeeeeeee." she jokes.

I nod to Dimitri and he whispers something to her before he leaves us.

"Are you going to tell me what I'm doing here?" she asks, her hands on her hips. I love it when she gets feisty. I pull her close to me, leaving the blindfold on and she squeaks in surprise at the movement. Her face tilts up by instinct and her lips are so close to mine, I can feel her breath on my face. She smells like peaches and cream, mixed in with a scent that is undeniably just her, and it's divine. I move closer and brush my lips across hers.

"You're awful with surprises, you know that?" I say.

"I never was any good with them," she says, her lips a breath away from mine.

"Time to learn then, hey," I murmur, taking a step back. I take her hand and lead her into the movie room, the lights are down and the movie is rolling with its opening credits. I remove her blindfold, and the gasp of wonder that escapes her makes me grin like a buffoon.

We flop down onto the sofas and she leans back onto me. My chin finds her shoulder and I wrap my arms around her, relishing her being here.

"Xander, this is so amazing! *The Notebook*?! How did you know?" she gasps.

"A little birdie told me this might be a favourite pastime of yours – this movie especially."

She turns and smiles at me. That smile is worth everything. It lights up her entire face.

DESCENT

She watches the film whilst I watch her. I observe the emotions play across her face, the depth of connection she has with the characters – it's fascinating. She feels so deeply; I hadn't realised just how deeply she felt. As it ends, I hug her tightly, kissing the top of her head and offering a silent apology for all she has been through in the last year.

"Do you think love like that exists, Xander?"

"I absolutely do. I know it can."

"Have you ever been in love before?" she asks, looking up at me with those big eyes of hers.

"Never before, but that could be us, Addie. Who knows how deep, how long our love could last. You just need to believe in it."

"I'm sorry, what did you just say?" she asks, her eyes wide with surprise.

I curse myself for letting that out – maybe she's not ready, but there's no taking it back now. "I love you, Addie. I should have said it before now, God knows it's been my reality for long enough. I love you."

She sighs contentedly and snuggles into me further. This next bit is going to suck.

"Addie, I need to tell you something." Pulling back from me, she stares up at me with those big grey eyes, and at the moment, I really hate my job. "I have to go away for a few weeks. I have a problem between a wolf pack and some humans. I can't tell you much, and I wouldn't go if I wasn't needed, especially since you just got back, but I have to leave."

"Leave? Now? Why can't someone else go?"

"I know, it couldn't be worse timing and I'm sorry."

"But I only just got you back." She says softly, looking down at her hands in her lap. She looks lost and scared and I hate it.

"I won't be gone long, I swear. I'll be back before you know it."

ADDIE

We've been here for two weeks now, and Rose is finally settled in, with Benny appointed as her personal guard and all round protector. It's kind of cute, and it's given me a lot more chance to train and not mope about the fact that I've not heard from Xander once since our night together when I got back. He didn't even bother to say goodbye. I know he told me he loves me, but what if he was just trying to placate me? He sure hasn't backed up his words, and everyone knows actions speak louder. He left, and my days have been empty other than training, and pretending to Rose like nothing's wrong.

Surprisingly it's not taken long to work out how to get around here. It's way easier than Kaden's place. I know it's wrong, but I kind of miss Kaden, Michael and Celeste. Of course, I know I shouldn't, I know I was their prisoner, but we still had some good times. I make my way to the room and take out my *Sai* and start practicing some combinations.

"You ready to get your ass kicked?" Dimitri asks as he enters the room with Aliana following closely behind.

"I am, but I'm hoping not to. Positive outcomes only right?" I laugh, pushing down any emotion other than my anger at Xander. I know it's irrational, but I think at this point, I'm allowed to be a little nuts. I try to focus on Dimitri in front of me and I just know I'm totally about to get my ass kicked.

I was right. Totally got my ass kicked, again. I make it back to my room and fall onto my bed. Every single muscle in my body aches, and every joint groaned on the walk back here. Once I lay down, I'm not sure I'll ever get back up. I hear voices approach my door, one of which belongs to a very excited Rose. I hold in the groan; I'm all pepped out right now.

My door bursts open and she floats into the room, followed by Benny and a blonde guy I don't recognise. I sit up, wincing, completely uncaring about meeting someone new while I'm sweaty and my hair is sticking to my forehead.

"Addie! Guess what! We're having a ball! A real life, fairy princess ball," she exclaims excitedly. I think she might actually explode with happiness, but oh wow, could I do without another freaking dress.

"That's awesome Rose. When is it?" I ask feigning interest.

Benny's smirk lets me know I'm not fooling anyone.

"It's in two weeks! I'm having a dress made. Queen Eolande is having her dress maker, Elaria, create something especially for me! I'm so excited!"

"I can see that," I say, laughing a little. "Rose?" I ask

"Yes?"

"Who's that?" I ask, pointing at the new blonde in the room.

"Oopsie! Addie, this is my father's squire, Christopher. Christopher, this is Addie, she is the one who found me."

"It's a pleasure to meet you," Christopher says, his voice as smooth as honey. He could give Xander a run for his money with a voice like that. If I wasn't so into that jerk, maybe I'd be swayed.

"Oh, believe me, Chris, the pleasure is all mine." I wink and Rose giggles.

"Come on then, let's start planning for this ball! First, let me shower then I'll meet you guys in the TV room?"

"Sure thing," Benny replies, ushering them out of the room, but stays behind.

"That means you too Benny."

"No need to be snarky, Addie. I'll go in a minute, but I wanted to speak to you. I know Xander's been gone pretty much since you guys got here, but you need to get your shit in line and pull yourself together. You're not this girl. The one who relies on a guy to be happy. You're not fooling anyone, and Rose is worried about you. Only, she's too scared to call you out in case that upsets you too, but I know you better than that. You've always respected the truth, so that's what I'm giving you. I don't know much about how you guys work, but I know you, Addie. Man up already.

"Is that all?" I ask, I'm beyond furious that he's calling me out, but I know it's not totally unfounded.

"Yeah that's all, now get your shower and get your head in the game. This isn't all about you."

Xander

It's been two weeks since I left Addie at the palace, but it feels like a lifetime. Everything I've had to deal with here has had my full focus, but it's also reminded me of my place in our world. Why I do what I do, why I fight for what I fight for. It's made everything that's been blurring my focus become clear. I do not live my life for me, I had my chance. It is my responsibility to set an example to those who I lead, those who I keep in line. To those who follow me. I've neglected all of this lately, and I need to stop being so selfish. I've seen first-hand these past two weeks what that sort of neglect can lead to.

I sit down at the table in the room given to me by the head of the Angulo pack who run this area. It's his mess I've been clearing up. I scrub my hands down my face before putting pen to paper.

Addie,

I can only imagine how angry you are at me right now for leaving you again so soon, and more so for not hearing from me. Things have been busy here, and this time apart has brought everything to focus. It's made everything clear to me, and I only hope that one day you can learn to forgive me.

Please know that I did not lie to you, I love you with every fibre of my being, but it is for the exact reason I need to stay away. I cannot be the man I need to be, the same man you fell in love with if I am always distracted, thinking of your safety and your wellbeing above anyone else's.

It hurts me to write this letter, just as I know it will hurt you to read it. I never intended to hurt you. You are everything. I have just come to realise it is selfish of me to have everything, when I am needed in so many places. Too much bad can come from such selfishness.

Just remember that I love you, and nothing will ever change that, but this world is bigger than us. We cannot be, we both have destinies bigger than us.

I miss you already.

Xander

I fold the piece of paper, and scrawl her name across the top.

"Take this to the Palace," I summon on of the guards on the team here with me. "Make sure you hand this to her yourself, do you understand?"

"Yes sir," he says, leaving the room and taking my heart with him.

ADDIE

. "Addie, you need to control yourself!" Dimitri yells at me across the room.

"Control myself? Are you being serious right now! You expect me to just carry on as if everything is okay, is that it? You're as bad as he is!" I shout back at him.

"It's fine, Dimitri," Aliana tells him as she dusts herself off after picking herself up off the floor. "I've got this. She's angry, we can use this."

"It is *not* fine, Aliana. She knows better, she was trained better." I pace back and forth as they talk. Xander finally reaches out to me, and he tells me that we can't be together, and I'm supposed to just keep going, act as if everything is peachy keen! I don't think so. Xander and Dimitri can go and hold hands in hell for all I care. Anger rushes through me and I don't want to control it. I want to break things. That's exactly why I came down to the training room.

Aliana comes at me again, and I let the anger wash over me, using it to fuel my fight against her. I hardly feel the blows she gets against me, everything fades away and it's like I'm not me anymore. I let go and everything goes blurry as I react and let me training take over. I grab Aliana's wrist and she jabs at me, using her momentum I pull her towards me, twisting her wrist and her arm until she's on her knees in front of me. I lean forward and hear a crunch before being tackled to the floor.

"Addie, what is wrong with you!" Dimitri roars and I come back to myself.

"What are you doing! I was winning!" I yell, struggling with him before throwing him off of me and standing up.

"You broke her god damn arm, Addie! She's one of us, do you even know how hard it is to do what you just did. Who the hell are you right now?"

I stagger back, I have no idea how I did that. I'm human, I should not have been able to do that. I look down

257

at my hands before looking over at them as Dimitri helps Aliana stand.

Who the hell am I?

ADDIE

The last week has passed in a blur. Preparations for the ball have been going on all around me, and I've gone through it all in a daze. Rose has been beyond excited about it all. Xander is back, and for the most part he's avoided me, except for once where I ran into him when I was with Aliana. I was checking in on her when she was with a healer, getting her arm sorted. He was with her when I arrived, but left shortly after. The next day my gown arrived for the ball, it's not the gown I've been going to fittings for, it's the complete opposite of that. It came with a note from Xander asking me to wear it, saying that he was sorry, that he was wrong. I can't bring myself to respond to him, but I hung the gown up regardless. I've avoided him at every opportunity, including leaving a room when he enters it. No-one said I was being mature about anything but I'm not sure exactly what I'm meant to do. I pull the dress out of the closet and hang it on the door.

It's stunning. The black material shimmers in the light, almost as if it were liquid. The corset bodice with purple crystals scattered across it, sparkles like stars. The skirt cascades in black ripples down straight and it's slashed with a thigh high slit. Exquisite – the Fae certainly have an eye for fashion. On the night stand is a matching lace mask, which will cover the top half of my eyes.

I close my eyes. Xander's generosity is too much, but now I'm here what can I do but as he asks? It's not as if I have anywhere else to go. I'm tired of fighting, and I miss him. I don't know who I am without him at this point, and while it scares me, I do love him. Who'd have thought? A vampire taking care of a human. It seems so unlikely, but I can't deny that it is true.

"What do you think?" he asks. One day soon, I'll get used to the fact he can move without a noise and stop jumping.

"It's stunning, Xander. It's like you took everything I could've asked for and made it a reality." It really is perfect. "I love it. Thank you."

"A thank you? From you? Well, *that* I didn't see coming." He winks, chuckling.

"Oh come on. I've not been that bad!"

"No?"

"Okay, so yeah, maybe a little. Anyway it's not like you don't deserve it... just... never mind. Just, thank you. Again."

He looks me over like he's trying to work out a puzzle then leaves. I sink onto the bed and feel the tension leave the room with him. I have no idea what is going on. I don't think I ever will. A gentle knock proceeds Dimitri.

"The door was open," he says.

"Yes, Xander just left." I huff and he smiles.

"You know he loves you? He just, well, I don't think he knows what to do about it. I don't think Xander has truly cared for someone in a long time. He's not... handling it well. Maybe he needs a push." He laughs knowing as well as I that nobody can make Xander do a god damn thing he doesn't want to.

"Oh, right, yeah, I'll use all those magic tricks being a human affords me and bend him to my will. I am after all the only non-magical species in the whole freaking world! He broke it off, then he sends me this," I say motioning toward the dress. "He's throwing out signals like crazy, and I have no idea what to make of it." I make light of it, but it's seriously frustrating. I feel like I was meant to be more than this. Be someone. But I'm *just* a human, and whilst that might have meant something in the Old World, I'm five hundred years too late to be important. I suppose that's the problem when all of your friends are supernatural.

261

DESCENT

"Believe me," Dimitri says fingering the fabric of the dress on the mannequin, "He wouldn't have had this made if he didn't care – and clearly I'm not the only one who can't wait for the ball." He winks, as he sweeps out of the room and I'm left feeling far more at ease. I turn to the dress and my ease wavers. It is a beautiful dress – and it's been made for me. There's something more about this, but I can't grasp it. Confusion ripples through me and my stomach lurches. Expectation? Yes, maybe that's it. Xander expects so much of me and I'm not sure I want to be held accountable to his expectations.

Ever since Kaden brought me home, life has been tripping me up. Each time I think I've found my feet, something else happens. I knew life would never be, *simple*, but I had hoped it might be a little more straightforward. Instead, I've been stuck to an eight-hundred-year-old Vampyr, who is grouchy as hell, but sweet as sin, too. I don't think many people have seen Xander's soft side, and hell if I'll be the one to share that secret. I just wish I got to see it a bit more. If he wasn't such an ass, maybe this wouldn't be so bad. I'm sure he has multiple personalities or something. I'm never going to work him out.

I get up and walk over to the dresser. It's one from the Old World, solid dark wood. It should be manly, but it's elegant and feminine. The string lights, which decorate the mirror make my skin look like it glows. I lift the mask to my face and tie the ribbon beneath my hair. I look in the mirror and I don't recognise myself. My big eyes sparkle against the darkness of the mask.

I walk to the Great Hall alone; I have no idea what I'm expected to do here. My aim is to stay out of the way, and maybe hide at the bar. I hope to god there's a bar! I walk up the steps towards the heavy velvet curtain and footmen. The master of Ceremonies is checking a list, preparing to announce the next gaggle of guests waiting impatiently to be let in. Fairies!

I spy Dimitri talking to one of the guards, and he winks at me as I approach. *Way to go filling me with confidence Dimitri!* Just, ugh. Time to pull up my big girl pants and do this. It's just a dance, and I'm wearing a mask. What's the worst that could happen? The Master of Ceremonies returns from his last guest announcement and looks at me. I smile sweetly and tell him my name, but stop him with a touch of the arm from leading me in. I really don't want a formal announcement of my arrival. I couldn't think of anything worse than all eyes turning to me. I take a deep breath as he pulls back the curtain.

DESCENT

It's another world. String lights flicker and dimly glow, illuminating the room, but making the shadows dance. They float across the room, under the magic of the Fae and it's beautiful. A fountain in the corner, trickles diamond water into a pool, creating a tinkling background noise that is strangely soothing. The tables are dotted amongst real blossom trees. *Only the Fae would make trees indoors for a party.* The extravagance is more than I could have ever imagined.

I've suddenly realised I've been caught in a dream, blocking the entrance. People have turned to look at me. God knows what I look like just standing here gawping at the room. I take a step in, but marble floors and six inch heels do not mix well. It's going to be a long old walk to the bar at the back of the room. I recognise Aliana behind the bar. She looks more like a pixie than a Vampyr, but she can totally kick my ass, as she has shown me regularly when I've trained with her, except for last time. I wince as I remember, she's forgiven me my act of crazy, or at least that's what she said after she healed up, and I hope to god she wasn't lying.

"Please, *please,* tell me you have something I can drink back there?" I beg her. I've got my puppy dog eyes out. I know she wants to be here about as much as I do.

"Anything for you, doll face." She smiles and pours me a drink. I have no idea what it is, but it tastes amazing. "You are rocking that dress by the way. I almost can't tell

264

you're a human." She laughs but I get the feeling that was exactly Xander's aim.

"Thanks, I think. And thank you again for not hating on me."

"It's nothing, Addie. Crap happens in training, I've been hurt worse and I know you didn't mean it."

"Thanks again," I take my drink and wander over to a corner table where no-one is sat. I avoid possible eye contact with the other guests by admiring the table decorations, calla lilies have been wrapped inside fishbowls, and teal stones give the effect of a river bed. Part of me is surprised the Fae didn't go all out and fill them with fish. Sitting down in the darkest corner I can find, I watch the Fae and the Vampyrs. They all drink, and dance as if the world isn't going literally to hell outside their walls. I mean, I totally get it, who doesn't want a night off, but really. The Demons are trying to rise up and humans are dying alongside the wolves trying to keep it all contained, and we're here having a party. It just feels wrong. I have no idea what the Demons want with me, I have no freaking clue, but they seem intent to take me, which is the only reason Xander keeps me close, and why Rose wants me to stay here. I know he wants me to tell him what they want. Ugh. Way to be the party pooper. I'm looking down into my drink when I feel warmth on my back. Xander.

DESCENT

"I wondered where I'd find you hiding, princess. Enjoying yourself?" He smirks.

"Oh, yeah. I'm the freaking life of the party!"

"Well, why don't you dance with me?" he asks

"Oh, hell no! I don't dance. And even if I did, I don't dance like you lot dance." No way. Not a chance. Not in this life time.

"Come on, Addie, just one dance? Did I mention that I'm sorry?"

"No, you didn't you jerk. You think you can tell me we can't be together, and then just show up here, demand I wear the most beautiful dress I've ever seen, and think everything will be okay again? It doesn't work like that Xander. We are not okay."

"I really am sorry, Addie. I never meant to hurt you, I had a moment of weakness. When the pressures from the rest of my life blinded me. I've been miserable without you, not being around you is like not being around the sun. I felt lifeless. Please forgive me, Addie? Let me make it up to you?"

He's being sweet again and it undoes me. I can handle him being a jerk, I can deal with jerks, but nice guys are so rare, I have no idea what to do. Wait. I'm lying. Yes, I do. I know I'm going to give in to him. He knows it, too. Smug ass he is. I can see it all over his face.

He puts his hand out to me without waiting for an answer, and I place my hand on top. My body knows exactly what I want, even if my head and heart doesn't.

"Fine! One dance, then I get to come back and sulk in my corner, this doesn't mean you're off the hook either!" I say. I don't know why I bother – we both know I'll do whatever he asks.

"Okay, just one dance."

He pulls me towards him, and I'm enraptured by his eyes. They're such a bright blue, they're such a contrast to his black hair and mask. He wraps one arm around my waist and takes the other hand. The piano in the background is haunting, and the voice of the Fae singing gives me goose bumps. Xander pulls me towards him, so close I swear I can feel him but I know we're not touching.

"I didn't know you could dance," I stammer. My sense, and apparently my words have disappeared.

"There's a lot you don't know about me, Addie. Just follow my lead." He sweeps me across the floor, and he moves with such grace that he almost makes me feel weightless. My head tips back as he spins me, and I feel like one of the women I've seen in the movies from the old days. He pulls me back to him and catches my eyes. I can't break from his gaze. I know I'm in trouble but I have no want or will to stop what's happening. I'm drawn to him like a moth to a flame, and I can't stop it.

DESCENT

He drops his hands to my waist and lifts me in the air, our eye contact unbroken. I have to remind myself to breathe. He slips me through his fingers and my hands come to rest on his biceps. He tenses beneath his suit sleeves. The whole room has disappeared and it's just us.

"Happy Birthday, Addie," he whispers, sending shivers down my spine. The sensations he brings out are more intense than anything I've ever known.

"How did you know?" I ask.

"I know more about you thank you think," he says as the music comes to an end. It's strange to think about everything that has happened since my last birthday. Last year I watched movies with Livvy, Tyler and Logan, and now... Well not one thing in my life is the same.

"Addieeeeeeeee!!" Rose squeal's my name as she rushes towards me. Being back around her own kind has been good to her, she looks so much better, and she's happier. I hug her tightly.

"Happy Birthday! I can't believe we're here, safe. It's more than I could have dreamed of; back with my kin, with my best friend by my side!"

"It's a good birthday, too," I smile. I look up and notice Xander has disappeared into the crowd. He's still here though, I can feel him.

"Are you okay? You don't look so good," she asks.

"I'm just a little cold, I'll be fine."

"Are you sure, Addie? You've gone really pale?"

"Of course, I swear it, I'm totally fine…" I say as I feel my legs give out beneath me.

This has got to stop happening I think as I come around. I open my eyes and groan. I'm back in my room at the Valoire palace and I can hear Xander and Dimitri outside my room. I push myself up and see Rose sat at the end of my bed.

"You really need to stop doing that, Addie!" she says launching herself at me. I laugh.

"Don't you laugh at me, missy! I'm not the only one who you worried! Xander looked as pale as a ghost when you passed out like that! He thought you'd been poisoned." She sighs wistfully, "No-one looks at me like he looks at you."

I roll my eyes. The more I've gotten to know her, the more I realise she's a diehard romantic. Who would've thought that after everything she's been through, she would still be peppy and optimistic.

"Xander should know better. He's seen me hit the deck harder than that. Hell, some of those were *because* of him!" I laugh. The door opens and Xander and Dimitri walk in. Dimitri stands at the end of the bed looking at me with that protective big brother look he's adopted since I got back.

"I'm fine, guys. No major panic. Just hadn't eaten enough, I guess." Xander sits down on the bed opposite Rose. His scowl has returned. Damn, I hate that scowl.

"Addie, you can't just dismiss this. Passing out is not normal. I've already called for the house medic."

I roll my eyes at him. "Xander, you're over reacting."

He cups his hand on my chin and looks deeply into my eyes, and I lean into him. He leans in so only I can hear him. "Addie, there is nothing I wouldn't do for you. Please, do this for me? Don't fight me – just this once?"

"Okay," I concede. "This once. When is she coming?"

"She's outside," Dimitri says, chuckling at the huff I let out. "He knew you'd give in." He winks and goes to the door to let the medic in.

"Come on in, doc. Don't worry, she won't bite. Well, maybe."

Chapter Eighteen

ADDIE

Three months later.

The past three months since my birthday have been a whirlwind. I've been training every day with Aliana, Xander and Dimitri. I've gotten so much better than I was. Quicker, more accurate — but I haven't told them I don't think that's just from my training. I've noticed a lot of changes happening to me since my birthday. I've been trying to keep them hidden, but I think Xander is slowly starting to catch on that something is different with me.

It started with small things, like noticing I could feel what people around me were feeling; even when they were trying to hide it. Then the voices started and I thought that maybe I was going mad. The only person I've dared tell is Rose. She desperately wants me to tell Xander, but I don't know how. What am I meant to do, just blurt it out? *Hi honey, I can hear what you're thinking.* Yeah that's going to go so well! Especially considering we promised no secrets, right around the time he made us official. Yeah that happened. Total swoon moment!

We were out walking in the gardens of the Valoire Palace, just talking. It was night but the moon shone so bright that it felt like twilight. His hand brushed mine, his fingers folding around my fingers. When we came to the edge of a lake, I couldn't resist emitting an unusual girlie squeal – he'd only gone and set up a blanket and spread little tea lights around a picnic basket. I remember being shocked he could be so sweet. He pulled me over to the blanket and sat me down beside him. He was giddy, and it was special to see him so unmasked. I knew I was possibly one of only a handful of people who he'd revealed his true self to – and I loved him for it. We feasted on what he called *chocolate covered strawberries*, which were apparently a delicacy of the Old World. He had tracked them down especially for me. He fed me between laughter, making it a messy affair. Using his thumb, he wiped away the juice that had escaped the corner of my mouth. I took his thumb in my mouth and such a small action caused a massive reaction inside. He growled and pounced on me causing me to fall. His hand flew out behind my shoulders, lowering me softly to the floor. His body fitting mine perfectly.

"Addie, you have to know that I will always catch you; I will always come for you. You are mine," he said just before his mouth crashed against mine.

That was two months ago, and since then it has been a whirlwind of sweet moments and passionate arguments. He can be so sweet but so thick headed, it makes me want to bash his skull in. This is why I haven't told him about the changes I'm undergoing. I don't know how he's going to react.

It's been hard enough talking to him about me not living with him here at the palace. He hasn't grasped the fact this isn't my home, and it never will be. I don't belong here, and I'd rather find out what the hell is happening to me away from the watchful eyes of the Fae. We've argued more times than I care to count about it. We're in the centre of the city, and there are apartments close where other humans live. I want a job. I want purpose and independence. At this point, I'd take working in the Academy as a Defence instructor! Just something to give me focus. I think he's coming around. It helps that Dimitri is on my side, plus Rose is going home in two weeks, which means there really is no reason for me to stay here. I look around the room which has been ours since our arrival. She refused to move to the palace without me, so I ended up here. The room is nice enough, but it's not home.

I fall back onto the bed and stare at the ceiling, when I hear my door open. I know it's Rose, another one of my new nifty weird traits is I can sense who is nearby. I can just feel them, though I'm learning how to shut it off unless I need it. It's work, but it's so tiring otherwise.

"You're projecting really loudly, Addie. You need to be careful, otherwise they're going to work out that something is different. You really should just tell them before they work it out themselves."

"I know, I know, but do you ever get the feeling they're hiding stuff from us, too? Like they know more than we realise? I catch weird feelings from them both. Like they're constantly waiting for something to happen. Like they know something is happening to me, but they're not saying anything."

"I don't know about that, but if they do, maybe they're waiting for you to say something first? Maybe they don't want to overwhelm you?" she says, as she floats over to my bed and sits opposite me. I shake it off, I've done enough wallowing already today.

"How are you? How was your training this morning?" I ask.

"Honestly? I don't know how they think I'm going to manage entering someone's mind while they're awake. I finally get a grasp on dream walking, and now they want me to do something else. I swear, if you were me, you'd have knocked that silly bitch the fuck out!"

274

My eyes widen so much they nearly fall out of my head. I don't think I've ever heard her swear before!

"Oh my god! I'm totally a bad influence on you!" I squeak and she laughs.

"I'm learning to channel my inner, Addie," she giggles, covering her mouth. The shy girl I know is back. She hops up and grabs my hand, pulling me to my feet.

"Anyway, come on lazy pants. I have something I want to show you," she says with a huge grin on her face, clapping giddily.

"Okay, okay. Where is it?"

"Oh, yeah you're going to need shoes."

I get myself together and follow her through the palace, out to the front where a car is waiting for us. She walks up to it and a guard appears, opening the door for her. She blushes as he smiles at her before thanking him and ducking in the car.

Here goes nothing.

We drive for maybe ten minutes when we pull up at a small single story, farm house. She giggles at me and bounces out of the car.

"Come on, slow poke! I need to show you!"

DESCENT

I follow her out of the car and up the stairs to the front door. The house stands alone, surrounded by fields, and a forest that seems to line the back and sides of the property. There's a wraparound porch with a swing bench to the left of the door.

"Rose, this place is beautiful. Who's is it?" I ask as she opens the front door. I follow her in and gasp. This place is beautiful. It's small and cosy, but with the small comforts like a TV and DVD player in the lounge, which also has a giant fireplace. I follow her through the rooms, kitchen, dining room, bathroom and two bedrooms all spanning across the one floor.

"This place is amazing, Rose. It's perfect," I sigh.

"I was hoping you were going to say that," Xander says from behind me. I squeak and turn to find him a breath away from me. He holds keys at eye height and I struggle to focus on them, because I can't stop looking at him. He still manages to take my breath away. "This place is for you. Well for us, if you want it that is?"

I squeal and jump into his arms. He catches me just like he promised he always would and kisses me. I swear I've never been so happy. I pull away from him and wrap my arms around his neck.

"Thank you, Xander! You have no idea what this means to me."

I hear Dimitri clear his throat and realise he's stood behind Xander.

"Don't I get a thank you for talking the big brute round, huh?" I jump down and hug him to.

"Thank you, Dimitri," I whisper.

"Anytime, Addie, you know I've got you. But you should know, one of us will always be here with you. Too much has happened to leave you out here on your own."

I cross my arms and bite down on my lip. I should've known it was too good to be true. I refuse to let this ruin my happy. I take a deep breath and let it out.

"Fine, but I'm decorating and none of you get to say anything!" I say, sulking. "And I get to hire whoever I want to help!"

Xander and Dimitri look at me sceptically, and I can see the excitement on Rose's face.

"Oh my gosh! We're calling Michael right?!" she squeals in excitement.

"No!" Xander roars. "The whole point of this is to keep you safe. If we invite them here, then there's no point in moving you here. We'll stay at the palace!"

I look at Rose who looks like she's going to cry. I walk over to her and hug her.

"You freaking idiot! Did you really need to yell at her like that?! I mean, seriously. Sometimes, you really don't have a clue do you! Get out. We'll follow you back later but right now, I can't even look at you."

DESCENT

I hear footsteps retreat before the door slams. I know Dimitri has gone with him and he'll make him calm down before I see him later. Men!

We moved in two weeks ago and surprisingly, we've not fought that much; when we do, it's mainly about the babysitters I endure when he's not here. Admittedly it's normally Dimitri or Ali, and I can handle that, but it's the others. The ones I don't know as well. They creep me out a bit but we're getting there.

I've been pottering about in the kitchen all day cooking. Dimitri and Xander are over for dinner tonight with Rose because she leaves tomorrow. The pain that thought causes, slashes through me, it's like losing Livvy all over again. She'll literally be half a world away, and I don't know when I'll get to see her again. I take a deep breath and push the pain down. I can get through this. She's cried almost every time I've seen her since she found out she was leaving. I know she's happy to get to see her family, but it's been so long, she's terrified. That's why I wanted to do this for tonight. I can't cook for shit, but I wanted her to know that we care.

I make sure nothing's burning and set the table. Xander made sure I have everything I could ever possibly want here. I'm pretty sure he's just using it as a distraction so I don't start looking for a day job. Apparently, it's safer if I'm home. What he doesn't know is that whatever is going on with me seems to be getting, well… more. Things are starting to be amplified, my sight, hearing, taste, touch; which has made some things *amazing*, but it means I've had to shield from him so much. I know for sure he knows something is going on, and I'm hoping he gets here soon so I can talk to him about it before the others get here.

My wish is granted when the door opens and I feel him. He doesn't seem angry, so it's better now than never.

"Addie? Are you here?"

"I'm in the kitchen," I reply, and grab him a bottle of blood from the fridge. I pop it in the microwave to warm a little. This had been another learning curve. Who would've thought living with a Vampyr, Fallen, whatever, would be so gross. I'm getting used to it, though. Better this than him chomping down on someone!

He walks in to the room as the microwave dings and grabs the bottle, using his spare arm to wrap me up in his hug. He tucks his face into the crook of my neck and breathes deeply. I sigh.

"I miss you," he says, and the guilt hits me hard. I've been hiding so much from him; I hadn't realised I was causing so much distance between us.

279

DESCENT

"We need to talk," I say.

He nods and leans against the counter. I pull away from him and wring out my hands. *Damn this is hard.*

"Okay, this is way harder than I thought it would be." I look up and see understanding eyes, encouraging me to tell him all of my secrets.

"I don't even know where to start, and I'm probably going to ramble but I need you not to get angry, okay? And don't speak until I'm done, otherwise I'll never get it out." I look at him, and he looks cautious but nods regardless.

"Okay, so ever since my birthday I've noticed things happening to me. I've been changing. It started small. I was faster, I could move easier in training, anticipate what was going to happen. Then it became more, I could feel people's emotions; at times, it was like they were going to take me over. Then there were the voices. I started being able to hear the thoughts of people around me. I learned how to put up a wall and keep people out, even that seemed to come too easy, and now there's more. I can see better, hear better. I can feel... more. I'm sorry I didn't tell you any of this before, I just didn't know how to, or what was happening, and I wanted to try and work it out on my own." I take a deep breath having just blurted that all out and look at the floor. I daren't look up, I can picture the anger swirling through those beautiful eyes of his.

"Addie, look at me," he commands softly. I look up and I don't see anger, but sadness and hurt. "You could've told me. I could've helped you with it all. I wish you could've trusted me enough to tell me what's been going on with you. I suspected something was wrong, but I didn't want to presume. Please always come to me with this stuff, okay?"

I nod and walk over to him where he holds out his arms to me. I squeeze against him and breath him in, relief floods me. He's not angry, but then...

"Why aren't you surprised?" I ask, looking up at his face. His shield comes down, his emotions shutting off. I hate it when he does that!

"I don't know what you mean. I'm trying to take it all in, understand it all."

"I know; I can sense it. But I can also sense you're not surprised. You knew something didn't you? Something you kept from me, something you're still keeping from me!" I shout.

I can't believe this! He knew, he knew this whole time. Is that why he got so close to me? Is this the real reason Kaden took me? I push away from him and distance myself from him.

"Addie, come on..."

"Don't you dare, Xander Bane. What do you know?" I ask.

"Don't do this, Addie," he replies.

"That is not an answer!"

"What do you want to know?"

"Everything! I want to know what you're hiding from me. Why didn't you tell me? What else is happening to me?"

"Addie, I can't, not yet. You don't understand."

"I understand perfectly," I say, anger clouding everything. "We're going to have this dinner for Rose, and we're going to pretend nothing's wrong. You should be good at that, your acting skills are on point, and then you're going to get out, do you understand me? I don't want to see you. I need some time alone."

"Addie, you know I can't leave you alone. I've got to go away with the team, but I'll make sure someone is here."

"Don't you dare. I don't want any of your so called protection. Leave me alone. I need some space. Does anyone else know? Does Dimitri know?"

The look on his face tells me everything I need to know and I run into the bedroom and lock the door behind me. A few seconds later, I hear him leave. Time and time again, they prove to me that I can't trust them. They keep things from me, and yet I keep letting them back in. Not again. I walk over to the mirror and wipe away the tears that have escaped, and put my happy mask back on. Tonight is about Rose and it will be perfect for her, tomorrow, I can let my life fall apart.

I finish prepping the meal just in time. Rose and her parents are standing on my porch and I'm in total awe. I have freaking Fae Royals in my house.

"Come in, please. It's so nice to meet you both," I say as Rose hugs me.

"Addie, stop being so polite it doesn't suit you, just be yourself," Rose says and I hear her mom and dad laugh. They've clearly been filled in.

"Addie, this is my mum and dad, Talia and Charles Frostheart. Mum and Dad, this is Addie," Rose introduces us officially, and her parents both hug me. This is so surreal.

"It's so wonderful to meet you at last, Addie, we've heard a lot about you!" Talia says, smiling at me. Her smile is so gentle and kind. I understand now why she is known as 'The Peoples Queen'. Her dad wraps me up in a giant bear hug.

"Thank you for bringing her back to us," he whispers, his eyes glassy when he pulls back.

"I'd do it all over again, if I had to. Rose is one of the best people I've ever known."

He pulls me close again and hugs me in the way only a dad can. I'm kind of jealous of Rose for having him. Maybe she'll share.

Xander and Dimitri arrive a little later, informing me the rest of the Elite are stationed around the property, along with the guards the Frosthearts came with, too. I feel bad they're outside, but I could never have cooked for everyone anyway.

"If everyone would like to take a seat, we're just waiting on one more and then I'll serve. Xander, can you get everyone a drink please?" I ask. I'm so not used to playing the host. I don't think I'm very well suited to it. Benny arrives a few minutes later looking dashing.

"Well, well, well. What do we have here, Benny boy. You scrub up good!" I say, bringing him in for a hug, laughing that he has to almost bend in half just so I can.

"Hey, Short Stack. I'm not late am I?" he looks nervous; I've never seen him look that way before.

"You're fine, Benny. They're going to love you; just like I do. Now come on!" I drag him through to the dining room and he sits down opposite Rose, just as I planned. Unfortunately, that means he's also next to Charles, and I think I can see him visibly shake with nerves. Poor guy.

Dinner goes well, and everyone seems to get on. Xander drops his dickish charm from earlier and acts like his normal self.

"So, I have something to announce," Rose says quietly, but it captures the attention of the room. She looks nervous so I smile at her to encourage her. I think I know what's coming, but she has to tell herself. She takes a deep breath and looks around the room. "It's been a long time since I've been home, and that is no-one's fault, but I want to know I have people there I can trust. That being said, Mum, Dad. I've chosen Benny to be my personal guard. Before you say anything, he has been trained by Dimitri and Xander, and he passed out into The Guard. He's a bloody giant, and I trust him, so I think he's the best person for the job." She doesn't take a breath and I see Benny pale. I'd laugh if it wasn't so tense.

"I think that's wonderful news!" Talia squeals in delight clapping her hands. Charles claps Benny on the back, and smiles.

"Well, I guess we best to get to know each other a bit better, son," he says, shaking Benny's hand. Benny gulps and nods and he can't keep the giggle in. Rose laughs, too.

"Well, now that's over with, does anybody want cake?"

The night wraps up and everyone prepares to leave, when Rose corners me in the kitchen.

"I can't believe you're not going to be with me every day. I don't even know how I survived without you, Addie. You're like the sister I always wanted."

"I'm going to miss you, Rose. I mean it, I know I can be a total bitch sometimes, but you're my best friend. Just don't forget me okay?"

"That is never going to happen! Once I'm home and settled in, you have to come and visit. Promise?"

"I promise." I hug her tight and try not to cry. I hate saying goodbye.

"Thank you for saving me, Addie," she whispers as she draws back, tears filling her eyes.

"I'd save you every time. Remember, you are worth everything. You are one of the best people I have ever known, and you are strong. They didn't take that from you, they couldn't, no-one can."

I hug her again before she turns and leaves, I hear her saying goodbye to everyone else then the door shuts. I can't believe she's gone – and Benny, too.

Last night was so surreal. Saying goodbye to Rose was one of the hardest things I've ever done.

Dimitri and Xander left shortly after she did, going wherever the hell it is they've got to go this time. Xander tried to talk to me again before they left, but since I refused to speak to either of them, he didn't have much luck. The look on Dimitri's face as I blocked him out was heart-breaking, but by that point, I was numb. Xander said he knew, too; another thing they both kept from me. I've had enough.

I've sat here all day in my very own pity party, watching *The Notebook* on repeat, wallowing in my own misery. This house might not be very big, but right now it feels huge. I get up and grab a drink, thank god for peach vodka! I'm pouring myself a glass when I hear a knock at the door. *Fucking babysitters.* I take a swig of the drink and savour the burn as it works its way down. I walk over to the door, ready to yell at whoever it is that's on my porch. Whoever it is knocks again.

"I'm coming!" *Jeez.*

I walk to the door and yank it open.

Holy fuck.

DESCENT

Chapter Nineteen

ADDIE

"Livvy?" I can't help but stare at her. She looks so familiar, but so very different all at once.

"In the flesh!" she laughs, but it sounds so hollow. I look at her closer, and while she's definitely Livvy, her eyes and cheeks are hollow and dark. Her hair still shines like it used to, but it's black now instead of blonde, and her skin is so pale against it. Whilst I know it's Livvy standing in front of me, it isn't my Livvy. My brain doesn't seem to be able to keep up with what I'm seeing. She tilts her head at me and a dark smile graces her lips.

"What's wrong, Addie? Didn't you miss me? Aren't you glad to see me alive, well not technically, but I'm here."

"It's not that Livvy, but you're not you anymore, are you? You're one of them, and that means you gave up your soul, so you can't be you," I say, still not really believing this is real.

I cast my eyes around the ground, searching out my babysitter. Freaking typical, always there until I need them.

"Ah, but I didn't. I didn't choose this, and I didn't give it up to him. It's still in here somewhere, I just don't engage with it unless I have to. All of that pain, that pathetic weakness, it does nothing but disable me in this life, but I'm still me Addie. Please believe me?" she pleads, and I want to believe her, really I do, but I don't trust so easy anymore. I learned my lesson.

"Why are you here, Livvy?" I ask. I'm sure my scepticism is all over my face.

"I'm here for you, Addie. I missed you, and he wouldn't let me out before, not until I could control myself, and I can now."

"Who is he?"

"*He* is Cole."

"Cole? Who the hell is Cole? You've been with him this entire freaking time?"

"Where else would I have been? And Cole is the Vampyr that syred me. He's out in the drift, not on either side of the war. I didn't even know there were Vamps like him until, well, until I became this."

"I thought you were dead Liv! Do you even understand that? DEAD! And now you tell me you couldn't even send me a letter to tell me you were freaking alive!"

"Oh, go do one! It's not like I haven't been dealing with shit, Ads! I turned into a fucking Vampyr! I've had so much going on in my head this past year, I couldn't have told you up from fucking down until a few months ago, when I started to gain some control over myself. Like I said, Cole wouldn't let me out, he wouldn't let me be around *anyone*. I've seen no-one but him for over a fucking year! And then, when he finally lets me come to you, *this* is what I get! Nice to see you too, Addie!"

"Don't be like that, Liv, you know me. You, more than anybody else, know me. You know I can't just accept this shit straight away! This is a lot! My best friend is a fucking Vampyr! And after everything I've dealt with since you died, or... whatever, none of it has made me more trusting, Liv. I wish Xander was here right now," I sigh.

"He's not here?"

"No, he got called out on some stupid secret mission with the rest of them. It's just me."

"Wow, I really have missed a lot. Want to try and catch me up some? We can make popcorn like we used to? I could do with some home comforts."

I soften at her request. Maybe she's just been dealt a shitty hand. I know she didn't ask to become a Vampyr, maybe she'll speak to Xander and ask to join the ranks. If she's still got her soul, surely it's a possibility?

"Yeah, sure, come on Liv, let me just pop some in."

We sit and talk for hours, about everything since she left. About Ty, and Xander and that giant mess – about the whirlwind my life has been since she left. I don't tell her about the big secret that seems to surround me because I haven't even begun to figure it out myself, and no-one seems to want to let me in on it.

I don't tell her about Xander, Kaden or the others either. I don't know what she knows, but that's not a secret I'm not about to tell. She doesn't tell me much about what she's been through but I can see the haunted look in her eyes so I don't press her.

"I can't believe it got so late! It almost feels like old times," I laugh.

"Yeah, it really did. I'm so tired! I didn't think I would be. Do you mind if I crash here?" she asks hesitantly.

"Erm, yeah I don't see why not. I'll grab you a t-shirt and shorts. Do you need anything else?"

"Do you have any blood?" I can almost feel her embarrassment at having to ask.

"Of course; I've got spares in case the guys are here. They're in the mini fridge over in the corner. Help yourself. I'll go and grab those bits for you."

I head out of the living room to my bedroom and grab some stuff for her. I take a minute, giving her chance to drink without me being around. I remember how long it was until Xander and Dimitri felt comfortable drinking around me. I thought it was funny, especially since I still donate once a month. I wait until I hear the bin lid and the sound of running water.

I wander through and give her the clothes before making my way to the bathroom to freshen up. It's so nice to have her back, if she's back.

I wish Xander was here. He'd quiet the voices in my head, he'd make me feel safe enough to work this out. I slip into his hoodie, which comes to my knees, and my pyjama pants before padding back to the lounge where Livvy is fast asleep on the sofa. I grab a blanket and drape it over her gently so as not to wake her. I do *not* want to disturb a baby Vamp's sleep; I enjoy breathing. I quietly make my way to our room and climb into bed.

I wake up to pain shooting from my neck and down my body but I can't move. I try to look around but everything is just a blur. Everything hurts so fucking much!

"Stupid, little bitch, you actually thought I came back for you didn't you? Why would I waste my time on a pathetic blood-bag like you? God knows why he wants you so badly but you're my way to climb, so I'm going to deliver you to him wrapped up in a nice little package. God, sitting through tonight was hell, listening to you whine about how shit everything has been for you. Well boo fucking hoo. I can almost guarantee that's going to be nothing compared to why he wants you."

I feel myself being picked up and bound, my ankles together and my arms behind my back. Fuck! Why did I trust her? Stupid, stupid, Addie. Fuck! Xander will think I've just left. What if he doesn't try to find me this time? Oh god, where is she taking me? Who the hell is *he* and what does he want with me? My mind whirls as my body is lugged outside and into the boot of a car. *Of course she has a fucking car. Bloody Vampyrs!* I can't make a sound. I close my eyes and try to pay attention to what turns she takes, but after a while, I can't keep up. It feels like I've been back here for hours and I still can't move. I hate feeling so helpless, and I don't know what she gave me, but it's kicking my ass. I feel my eyes start to droop, and as much as I want to fight it, it's a losing battle.

I wake up and all I feel is pain. It takes me a second to remember, and then it hits me. Livvy. I open my eyes and realise I can actually move again, though the tightness on my wrists and ankles lets me know I'm still bound. I'm lying down on a muddy, dirt floor, in a room that looks little better than a cave, except for the bars that keep me in here.

"Hello! Is there anybody there?" I try to shout out, but it comes out a croaky whisper. I really need some water. I tense as I hear footsteps approach the room I'm in. I sit up and put my back against the wall in an attempt to be as far away from whomever that is as possible. I sit and wait what feels like forever until I see a man, a Vampyr, I mentally correct.

"Hello, Addie, it's nice to finally meet you," he says

"I wish I could say the same, but one, I don't know who the fuck you are, and two, I'd really rather not be bound in a muddy cell, thanks." I don't bother to keep the venom from my voice. I want to be home with Xander and Dimitri.

"Now then, young lady, that's no way to speak to your host. If you'd have asked, I'd have gladly told you my name. I'll overlook it this time. My name is Cole."

"Then you're not a Vampyr, Livvy told me you syred her?"

"Yes, well, Olivia does tend to have a way with words doesn't she? Talented little bitch, I didn't Syre her but she is one of my best and brightest new recruits. I think she's with your friend, Logan, but I'm guessing from the look on your face she didn't tell you about him either."

I can't work out if he's telling me truth, or who the hell he is, and I think that's pissing me off more than the fact that I'm here.

"Uh-huh. If you say so, but erm, what exactly are you?"

"Ahhh, I was wondering when you'd get to that part. Well my dear, I am Cole, but most people know me as the Demon King, but then I know you know a little more about me than most people from The Academy. Kaden did so well with his little mission until... well yes, you'll see soon enough," *shut the hell up! No way!* "Shocked you again didn't I? Well one more for you at this point won't hurt I suppose." His smirk winds me up.

"Oh just spit it out, whatever bullshit it is," I yell at him, well I try, stupid croaky voice. I'm going to kick Liv's ass as soon as I get the chance.

"Oh it's not bullshit, my dear, as you so eloquently put it. What I'm about to tell you goes against everything you've ever been told, but it's one hundred percent truth."

He takes a breath and pauses, watching me to see if I believe him. "You are truly one of a kind, Adelaide, and that's why I've persisted in getting to you – so I can tell you the truth. You're not human, Addie. I can see your mind ticking away. You've noticed something isn't right and soon you'll see how this fits. You're Fallen, Addie."

"What?! No fucking way. That can't happen."

"It can, and it has. I know it for a fact."

"How could you possibly know that? If I even believe it's true."

"I know Addie, because I'm your Father."

SLOANE MURPHY

To be continued…

DESCENT

THE IMMORTAL CHRONICLES

Addie

In that one moment everything changed. Everything I
thought I knew shattered with just a few words.
Who knew the truth could be so devastating?
I need to decide which side to take. But can I even trust
myself?

Xander

She's gone, but I'll scorch the earth to find her if that's
what it takes.
I'll call upon friend and foe for the battle that is to come.
The fires of hell couldn't keep me from her and whoever
thinks they can take what is mine, is going to regret it for
all time.

One thing is for sure. The Crash could ruin us all.

SLOANE MURPHY

Also by Sloane Murphy

The Immortal Chronicles

Descent

Crash

Soar

Rapture

Of Fire & Frost

A Princess's Duty

A Kings Oath (Coming Soon)

Standalones

When We Fall

AUTHOR NOTE

There are so many people I need to thank in here, but I don't want to waffle on for hours.

Thank you to *him,* for putting up with my random moments of inspiration, where diving for my laptop in the middle of dinner became the norm. For encouraging me to do this, and to stick at it. For being my sounding board at ass o'clock, because I can't decide whether or not to scrap something, or to play with it until it works. I'm pretty sure without that, this wouldn't exist.

To Ali & Rose, my personal whippers and word hogs. I'm not taking sides; you can fight over him all you like, aha! Seriously though, thank you so much for taking this journey with me, reading through some absolute rubbish and telling me when to bin it.

To Jenn, for always having a supportive word when I needed it, even when you didn't know it.

To Jade, for putting up with my random acts of crazy about this cover. I absolutely love it, and I admire your genius immensely. ~~I swear to never put you through that again.~~ I'd love to say that, but I'm not going to lie. Thank you for getting to know Addie and showing her so beautifully.

To Annie & Alex, for always having my back, or a shovel, whichever is needed first.

And finally, thank you to you. Thank you for taking a chance on this book. Thank you for wanting to get to know these characters. I hope you love and cherish them as much as I do.

DESCENT

Thank you so much for taking a chance on Addie & Xander. I hope you enjoyed reading them as much as I enjoyed writing them.

If you'd like to leave a review on Amazon, please do! Reviews make this indie super happy!

Come & say hi, and to keep up with news on Addie and Xander here

Facebook: https://www.facebook.com/sloanemurphybooks

Twitter& Instagram: @author_sloanem

Come join my Facebook reader group for exclusive excerpts & special giveaways.

https://www.facebook.com/groups/SloaneMTheFallen/?ref =bookmarks

Made in the USA
Monee, IL
07 May 2020

30154242R00180